To Carol Kohan

from

CHINA MENDING

CHINA MENDING
A guide to repairing and restoration

ECHO EVETTS

With a Foreword by
JOHN P. CUSHION

FABER & FABER
LONDON AND BOSTON

First published in 1978
by Faber and Faber Limited
3 Queen Square London WCIN 3AU
New and revised edition first published
as a Faber Paperback 1983
Filmset and printed in Great Britain by
BAS Printers Limited, Over Wallop, Hampshire

© Echo Evetts, 1978, 1983

British Library Cataloguing in Publication Data

Evetts, Echo
China mending.
1. Pottery—Repairing—Amateurs' manuals
2. Porcelain—Repairing—Amateurs' manuals
I. Title
738.1′4   NK4233
ISBN 0-571-13058-5

Contents

Acknowledgements   *page* 11

Note to U.S. readers   12

Foreword   13

1. Introduction to china repairing   15

2. The work room   18
work space and lighting, ventilation, furniture.

3. Tools and equipment   20
tools, equipment and miscellaneous items.

4. Materials   28
adhesives; fillers; materials for cleaning and preparation;
modelling and moulding materials; glaze mediums and
their solvents, paints and pigments; gilding; surface
finishing; miscellaneous materials.

5. Protection while working   36

6. Choosing the first project   37

7. Cleaning and preparation   39
epoxy resin adhesives on porcelain; epoxy resin
adhesives on pottery; shellac on pottery and porcelain;
animal glues; rubber cement; cellulose adhesives; old
paints and varnishes; stains; removal of rivets; other
stains; washing; labels.

8. Putting the pieces together   45
Two-Tube Araldite; Ablebond 342-1 epoxy resin; polyvinyl
acetate emulsion; cyanoacrylate resin; bonding with Two-
Tube Araldite; the sprung or warped join; multiple breaks;
bonding with Ablebond 342-1; bonding with cyanoacrylate
resin adhesive; bonding with polyvinyl acetate emulsion.

9. Filling in, building up and reinforcing   59
a simple filling-in exercise; filling cracks; supports for
edge chips; filling in pottery; moulds to assist filling in
missing pieces; rubber latex moulds; direct modelling;
silicone rubber moulds; two-piece moulds; reinforcing;
dowelling; pinning.

10. Colour-matching, painting and glazing   79
painting materials; to bake or not to bake; the first
exercise in painting; hints for successful painting;
painting with Chintex; painting with Bedacryl 122X
(Acryloid B48N); spray-painting or airbrushing; a
problem; decoration.

11. Gilding   93
gold leaf; tablet gold; bronze powders; lustre wares.

12. Surface finishing   97

13. Restoring a porcelain pastille burner   99

14. Restoring a Chelsea plate   106

15. Restoring a Derby vase   111

16. Restoring a Creamware centrepiece   116

17. Restoring a tin-glazed earthenware cup   121

18. A word on restoring T ang pottery   125

19. Porcelain dolls' heads   130

Glossary   132

Reference books   136

Alphabetical list of materials, tools and
equipment   140

Alphabetical lists of suppliers   150

Index   154

Illustrations

Photographs

1. Cabbage-shaped pot before bonding   *page* 47
2. Cabbage-shaped pot, repair   47
3. Cabbage-shaped pot, the finger test   48
4. Chinese Export plate   51
5. Chinese Export plate, repair, stage 1   51
6. Chinese Export plate, repair, stage 2   52
7. Damaged pastille burner   99
8. Pastille burner, repair, stage 1   101
9. Pastille burner, repair, stage 2   101
10. Pastille burner, repair, stage 3   101
11. Pastille burner, repair, stage 4   101
12. Pastille burner, repair, stage 5   103
13. Pastille burner, the completed repair   104
14. Chelsea plate with broken rim   106
15. Chelsea plate, repair, stage 1   108
16. Chelsea plate, the completed repair   109
17. Derby vase with handles missing   112
18. Derby vase, repair, stage 1   113
19. Derby vase, repair, stage 2   115
20. Derby vase, repair, stage 3   115
21. Broken Creamware centrepiece   116
22. Creamware centrepiece, repair, stage 1   117
23. Creamware centrepiece, repair, stage 2   119
24. Creamware centrepiece, the completed repair   119

25. Tin-glazed earthenware cup in poor condition   *page* 121
26. Tin-glazed cup, repair, stage 1   122
27. Tin-glazed cup, repair, stage 2   123
28. Tin-glazed cup, the completed repair   124

Drawings

1. Tools for measuring and modelling   21
 2. Labelling   28
 3. Removing old rivets   42
 4. A sprung break   50
 5. Applying adhesive to a multiple break   52
 6. Applying de-ionized (or distilled) water   57
 7. A use for Scotch tape   61
 8. Rubber latex mould   70
 9. Preparing a Plasticine 'box'   71
10. A completed Plasticine 'box'   73
11. Dowelling a plate   75
12. Modelling a forearm   77
13. Mixing pigments   82
14. Pencilling in a repeated pattern   90
15. Choosing the right brush   91
16. Cutting gold leaf   94

Acknowledgements

My thanks are due to a number of people who gave encouragement, advice, or information: Dr Robert Organ of the Conservation-Analytical Laboratory, Smithsonian Institution, Washington, D.C., U.S.A.; Mr John Cushion, lately of the Victoria and Albert Museum; Miss Judith Larney, in charge of Ceramic Conservation at the Victoria and Albert Museum; and Mr Jens Yow of the Pierpont Morgan Library. Mr and Mrs Price Glover generously lent the Leeds Creamware centrepiece and the blue and white tin-glazed cup for photographing. Mrs Sarah Gleadell was a splendid critic, and my sister, Deborah Evetts, who undertook the onerous task of photographing the restoration in progress, helped in many other ways. My brother Jonathan Evetts had a very good idea and Dorothy and Douglas Adams gave help and information unstintingly.

Note to U.S. readers

U.S. equivalents are given in
brackets throughout the text. The
alphabetical list of materials, tools and
equipment on page 140 shows American
products, and there is a list of U.S.
suppliers on page 151.

Foreword

There is little doubt that today the most popular form of collecting in the field of antiques is that associated with decorative earthenwares, stonewares and various types of porcelain. It is a subject in which both enthusiastic amateurs and experienced collectors can acquire pleasing pieces according to their financial means: the more moderately priced wares of recent years or the rarer and usually more expensive examples of the eighteenth century or earlier. The older the wares, the more likely it is that such vulnerable material will have suffered at least some minor damage; in fact to find a collector's item of the eighteenth century, or earlier, in mint condition is often a clue to its being a later reproduction.

Present-day high costs of materials and labour have put the use of professional services far beyond the purses of many in almost every trade or craft, necessitating today's popular vogue for 'do-it-yourself'. With competent and expert guidance, this same trend can well apply to the repair and restoration of all forms of ceramics. This new book by Echo Evetts gives all the necessary advice.

To suggest that any person can easily and successfully repair pottery or porcelain would be an extravagant claim. There are many unfortunate folk who are prepared to admit that they are 'hopeless' at using their hands for any delicate operation; such people will unfortunately have either to buy perfect wares, tolerate imperfect pieces, or pay dearly to have them expertly restored.

Prior to restoring ceramics Echo Evetts had the advantage of an ideal art-school training, including modelling, which plays such an important part in the satisfactory repair of earthenware or porcelain figures. There are many ceramic restorers in business today, some good, some bad, but all usually asking prices for repair and restoration which in most instances are far beyond the sale-room value of the piece involved. Many good restorers prefer to keep the various methods and materials they use a closely guarded secret, but not so Echo. In this volume she has generously and successfully made every effort to help ceramic restorers, both new and experienced, to achieve the same excellent results which she herself has been producing over many years, first in England and more recently in the United States of America, where her skills have been called upon by major American museums and art galleries.

The repair of pottery and porcelain can be carried out with various aims. Museums are usually content to have the object look pleasing to the visitor without a great amount of 'overpainting'—a device often used to help carry the eye away from the defect; other repairs are made to restore an article to its initial useful purpose. Echo Evetts helps the reader to achieve any of these desired results, aided with illustrations where necessary.

I am often asked for advice on how to learn to repair ceramics and, apart from recommending a few private courses and evening classes, this has been a difficult question to answer. This new book should now supply the requirements of all those prepared to acquire with patience a new and rewarding skill.

JOHN P. CUSHION

1. Introduction to china repairing

Unlike bookbinding, embroidery, and pottery-making there have been, until recently, few books on china mending. Anyone attempting to unravel the mysteries of the craft found himself confronted with a myriad conflicting ideas. How should the would-be restorer mend his favourite Derby figure or fill in a chip on a teapot lid?

Now, however, collectors may choose between taking their treasures to professional restorers or repairing the pieces themselves, in their own homes. With the help of enthusiastic museum conservation officers, national and international organizations, magazine articles and a few books, the mysteries *are* being unravelled. First of all, it is important to understand the difference between conservation and restoration. Conservation is the term used to describe the type of work carried out on historic and priceless pieces in the museum conservation laboratory. Here it is essential to do the *minimum* amount of repairing, in order to display the *maximum* area of the original piece. Outside the museums, those who handle pottery and porcelain are variously known as restorers, repairers or menders. The aim of this book is to show the beginner the rudiments of china repairing, in the simplest possible way.

It is necessary to use good quality materials, and the correct tools. The beginner will need also to cultivate his artistic sensibility, manual dexterity, and **patience**. There are several things the learner can do to increase his knowledge of pottery and porcelain and associated subjects—all invaluable in ceramic restoration.

1. Read books on art, art history, and the pottery and porcelain factories, as well as the history of ceramics.

2. Attend lectures at the local museum. In some areas there

are evening classes in repairing ceramics, and it is always worth while investigating them. Pottery classes, too, are useful because they teach how a pot is shaped, the different ways of decorating, glaze colours, and firing temperatures. A good way to develop skill with the hands is to take a course in clay modelling, where there is a live model, but instead of modelling a complete figure, concentrate on individual limbs. The restorer will never have to make a complete figure but arms, hands, fingers, and sometimes legs and feet, will be missing from the figurines brought to his workshop.

A good sense of colour is essential. Colour-matching is an important part of restoration. Become colour-conscious; train the eye to recognize good colour combinations in such everyday things as flowers, clothes and furnishings.

One of the things which beginners find difficult is learning to handle ceramics, especially the more valuable pieces, without fear of breaking them. The only way to overcome this is frequent contact. Always sit down so that the lap, or a table, stands between the object and the floor. As time passes, handling even really valuable objects becomes second nature. Even so, the restorer must never lose sight of the fact that the things he is working with *are* breakable and must be treated accordingly. Make it a rule never to have more than the piece in process of being restored on the work bench or table. A second piece can be so easily knocked off by an elbow or a dropped tool, or banged against another object. As soon as a stage has been completed on a particular piece, put it out of harm's way in the cupboard or on a shelf.

Aim high—buy the best quality materials and work on good pieces as soon as sufficient confidence has been gained. Use the airbrush when absolutely necessary: for handles and arms, and for some large background areas where hand painting would take too long and possibly not provide a fine and even enough surface. It is very important to develop the hand painting technique at the beginning because it will take time to perfect, even for those who have experience of other types of painting.

Start on simple things such as Staffordshire pottery figures and groups, the ones with bright blobs of royal blue, orange, brown and green. They are fun to work on and satisfying results can be achieved with the minimum of pain for the beginner. Soft-paste porcelains, such as Chelsea, Derby and Bow are all easier to work on than, say, Chinese Export porcelain. The higher the temperature at which the clay was fired, the more difficult it is to imitate the surface.

Perhaps it should be explained that hard-paste, or true porcelain, is fired at about 1,450°C (2,642°F) and soft-paste porcelain is fired at 1,200°C (2,192°F) to 1,250°C (2,282°F).

2. The work room

Work space and lighting

China repairing can be done at home because relatively few pieces of large equipment are needed and quite a small room can be converted into a studio. A north-facing window provides the best light by which to match colours. The other processes can be accomplished satisfactorily by artificial light, using a flexible lamp with two 15 watt bulbs, one slightly warm in colour, one slightly cool.

Ventilation

An important consideration in the studio is the ventilation. Since solvents, glazes and some adhesives give off unpleasant and in some cases harmful fumes, it is imperative to have good air circulation, either from open windows or an extractor fan. It cannot be too strongly stressed that it is dangerous to work with solvents in a poorly ventilated room.

Furniture

The essential pieces of furniture for a studio are a table, a chair, a cupboard or open shelving, a small trolley, a pedal rubbish bin, and a sink.

THE TABLE must be sturdy and absolutely firm, for the safety of the objects and to avoid the irritation of working on a rickety surface. The recommended[1] width is 80 cm (32 in) and the height 70 cm (28 in). The length can vary, depending on the availability of a trolley for tools and materials, but 150 cm (5 ft) is a useful size. The surface *can* be wood, but this is not ideal; it is difficult to keep clean, becoming stained and unpleasant-

[1] See R. M. Organ, 'Scientific Conservation of Antiquities', Smithsonian Institution. 1968. Page 8.

smelling with constant use. White Formica is easy to clean, looks nice and is satisfactory as a work surface.

THE CHAIR The recommended[2] height for the chair seat is 43 cm (17 in) and the depth 38 cm (15 in). To make it more comfortable for the restorer who is taller than average, put a 2·5 cm (1 in) thick mat under the feet, or for one who is short, a firm, 2·5 cm (1 in) thick cushion on the seat.[3] It is important to be comfortable.

THE RUBBISH BIN The bucket-shaped container inside the rubbish bin should be made of metal. Line the bucket with a plastic bag and change it every day.

THE SINK If a sink with a draining board is not available, a wash-basin with a small table beside it will suffice. Always use a plastic bowl to prevent the objects from coming in contact with the hard surface.

THE CUPBOARD AND OPEN SHELVING Ideally, tools and materials should be kept in a cupboard. Work in progress will dry best on open shelving.

METAL CUPBOARD For the safe storage of inflammable solvents, a metal cupboard is recommended. The odours will also be contained.

SMALL VACUUM CLEANER To clean up after dirty jobs, such as sanding. The studio must be kept as free of dust as possible to protect wet, painted surfaces.

[2,3] See R. M. Organ, 'Scientific Conservation of Antiquities', Smithsonian Institution. 1968. Page 8.

3. Tools and equipment

There is a great deal of truth in the saying that the workman is as good as his tools. To be able to turn to a quality tool, which is also the correct one for the job, is a very satisfying experience for all craftsmen.

This chapter is devoted to a complete list of tools and equipment, with a description of the uses for each one. An alphabetical list of names and addresses of suppliers, and a second alphabetical list of tools, equipment, and materials (see next chapter), will be found at the back of the book.

Some of the tools are essential and they are marked with an asterisk; the rest may be acquired as they are needed, or when funds permit. The suppliers named have good-quality tools and, although some may be expensive, it is important to start with the best obtainable because they will last longer and give far more satisfactory service. Hints on cleaning and storing are also given; nothing shortens the effective life of a tool faster than lack of care. Those who possess a tool box may find several tools which will serve until new ones can be acquired.

Tools

PAIR FINELY POINTED TWEEZERS* For removing pieces of dust which have blown onto a painted surface and for handling minute chips during the bonding process. Protect the fragile tips with a short length of narrow plastic tube, and store separately.

PAIR HEAVY-DUTY TWEEZERS Preferably with curved ends for handling cotton wool swabs and lifting other objects. Protect the tips.

PAIR SMALL CALLIPERS For measuring when modelling. Protect the fragile points.

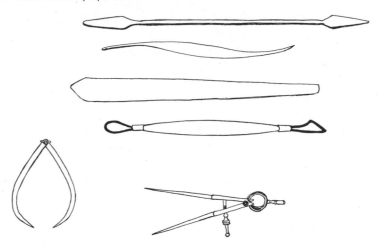

Fig. 1. Tools for measuring and modelling

PAIR DIVIDERS As callipers.

PAIR SMALL CURVED SCISSORS* For cutting tape, paper or tissue-backed gold leaf. Keep well sharpened and store separately.

PAIR MEDIUM SCISSORS* For cutting rags, etc.

HOLDER NO. 3* for small scalpel blades, and HOLDER NO. 4* for large scalpel blades.

SCALPEL BLADES* For many scraping, cutting and carving jobs. Buy them by the dozen, one or two shapes to fit each holder. Each restorer has his own opinion as to the best shapes. Keep clean. Sharpen on Carborundum stone.

SINGLE- AND DOUBLE-EDGED RAZOR BLADES* The latter to be used with extreme care. All blades should be kept in a box. Do not leave lying around.

A STEEL RULER Can be useful.

PENCILS* For marking distances in repeated patterns, and marking out complete patterns, when painting.

PEN AND PAD* For making notes on the work, and for keeping a shopping list of materials that are running low.

A METAL SPATULA For mixing adhesives, mixing glaze

medium with colours and sometimes for modelling. Always clean with appropriate solvent.

BOXWOOD MODELLING TOOLS* In several shapes, for modelling, mixing, and filling in. One would do at first. Rub with fine sandpaper to make more pliable when very new, and to remove uneven edges after long use. Clean with methylated spirits (ethyl alcohol).

WIRE MODELLING TOOLS For cutting Plasticine and other modelling materials. Buy a large size for cutting lumps from the main block, and the smallest size for use in direct modelling.

HAND DENTAL TOOLS IN ASSORTED SHAPES For scraping out old rivet holes, occasionally assisting in modelling in small, awkward places, and other uses which the restorer will discover as he progresses. These can be bought from dental suppliers, but expense can be avoided if your dentist can be persuaded to part with some of his old tools!

TWO PALETTE KNIVES* One long and straight, one short and angular. For mixing, scraping, stirring and many other uses. Clean with appropriate solvent. Store in box or upright jar.

SABLE PAINT BRUSHES* Artist's quality sable water-colour brushes are the most suitable. The restorer must choose the size of brush which will best suit his way of working, but Nos. 0 to 4 or 5 are the most useful sizes. Occasionally a 00 can be used for very fine lines or minute detail. Brushes larger than No. 5 become unmanageable when loaded with glaze medium.

AGATE BURNISHER (Since gilding is one of the more difficult processes, this could be left until required.) For burnishing gold leaf to increase the gloss and help to blend with surface of original leaf. Very fragile, store with agate wrapped in soft fabric and keep away from other tools.

SET OF GRAVERS* For sharpening detail on objects cast in Araldite (Devcon Clear, Epotek 301 or R.P. 103) composition. *They can also be bought separately*, with or without handles. Clean with solvent. Sharpen on Carborundum stone. Store separately: they become blunt very quickly.

SET OF NEEDLE FILES* To assist in shaping and modelling dry composition. These come in coarse, medium and fine grades.

Start with a set of medium files (*or buy them individually*), and acquire the coarse and fine grades later if needed. Needle files are very fragile. If bought as a set they will probably come in their own plastic case which is an advantage. After each use, clean very gently with a soft brush.

A FEW RIFFLER FILES, CURVED AND STRAIGHT For shaping dry composition. Clean with wire brush and store separately.

A WIRE BRUSH* For cleaning files.

A PAIR OF 12·5 CM (5 IN) TOP CUTTERS (END CUTTERS)* For cutting dowelling wire. Also useful for breaking plaster support away from filled rubber latex moulds.

A PAIR OF 12·5 CM (5 IN) FLAT, LONG-NOSED PLIERS Not essential, but useful for bending wire. Clean all pliers with wire brush.

A PAIR OF 12·5 CM (5 IN) ROUND-NOSED PLIERS Not essential, but useful for bending wire. Larger or smaller pliers and top cutters may be purchased to suit the individual restorer's needs.

HACKSAW BLADES* For cutting old rivets in half when they cannot be dislodged with pliers.

FILE, LARGE MEDIUM CUT* For roughening surface of dowelling wire and smoothing the ends of dowels.

A SMALL METAL VICE To clamp to the work bench for holding dowelling wire and occasionally other objects where two free hands are needed. Line jaws with leather.

TRIANGULAR-SHAPED CARBORUNDUM STICK (CARBORUNDUM SLIP)* Used occasionally to make slots in porcelain to provide a better 'purchase' for the composition, for instance, where it is not possible to drill for a dowel. Store separately to avoid damaging the edge.

A FINE CARBORUNDUM STONE (ARKANSAS STONE)* For sharpening gravers, scalpels and other edges. Use with oil. Keep free of dust by storing covered.

PIN VICE To measure the depth when drilling holes for dowels. A piece of thin wire is set into the pin vice with the required length protruding.

DOWELLING WIRE* Gauges 11G to 18G or 19G in half hard brass, or soft stainless steel. Wire is used to strengthen heavy objects by being cut to size and set into drilled holes with Araldite composition. Single pieces of wire are set into shoulders or wrists, or wherever support is needed for free-hand modelling.

SHEET BRASS To make tube dowels for hollow parts needing strong joins.

ELECTRICAL WIRE (TIE WIRE)* This is a tinned copper wire which comes on wooden reels. Three useful gauges are Nos. 30G, 33G and 38G; or use finer or heavier as required. Used as support instead of dowelling wire when modelling very small objects such as fingers where it would be impossible to drill holes, and for various binding operations. The 30-gauge can be used to bind together the two filled sections of a silicone rubber mould.

AIRBRUSH* For spray-painting larger areas of restoration. Also for painting arms and handles where it would be difficult to achieve an even surface by hand painting. Powered by a compressor, the airbrush looks like a small gun and has a colour cup attached. Ask also for a spatter cup for special effects.

COMPRESSOR* To provide air pressure for the airbrush. It can be either foot or electrically operated, the latter being the more expensive machine. The foot operated one is perfectly adequate for the restorer's purpose, but it does mean constant attention to the gauge, whereas the electrically-powered compressor automatically builds up the pressure as soon as it falls below the required level.

DE-IONIZER Elgastat B. 114, with five cartridges (DE-MINERALIZER Illco-Way Universal Model). For supplying de-ionized (demineralized) water, which is purer than distilled water, and is used wherever water is mentioned in the text. However, the de-ionizing unit is an expensive item for the beginner and can be omitted in favour of distilled water, until the budget permits.

FLEXIBLE SHAFT DRILL* While an electric drill is also an expensive piece of equipment, it is extremely useful and will be needed as soon as the restorer starts working on large pieces which require strengthening with dowels, and when the time comes to model hands and arms and other protruding areas over a metal pin. Holes are drilled into the ceramic with diamond-tipped instruments set into the electric drill. Another use for the drill is grinding down composition fillings but this must be done with the utmost care—if the drill should slip a great deal of damage can be done to the surface of the glaze, and it is very easy to grind down the filling further than is needed. Eventually it may be necessary to acquire a drill which can be converted to either a vertical drill on a drill stand or to a horizontal drill with a bench clamp.

DIAMOND-TIPPED AND CARBIDE INSTRUMENTS* In a variety of shapes including a point to start holes. For use with the electric drill to make holes for dowels; for grinding, cutting, smoothing, and many other little jobs which will crop up as the work progresses.

SET OF GRAMME SCALES* These will be necessary when measuring adhesives such as Araldite AY 103 and Hardener HY 956 and Ablebond 342-1 epoxy resin, parts A and B.

LAMP* Flexible arm lamp with clamp to enable it to be fixed to the work table.

Miscellaneous items

PLASTIC KITCHEN BOWLS* Ranging from the size used for washing-up, to small ones with lids. The former are used for washing purposes to protect the ceramic from contact with the sink. The smaller ones are for soaking small objects and chips, and various other uses will be found.

KITCHEN FOIL* Used as a cover for the washing-up bowl when it is being used for soaking ceramics in acetone, which would evaporate if left uncovered, and when using swabs of hydrogen peroxide to bleach out stains and cracks.

OLD TEA-TOWELS* These are useful for draining objects after washing. It is usually better to drain rather than to dry so that pieces of lint from the towels do not become caught in the ceramic.

RAGS* Silk and fine cotton rags are a 'must'.

SMALL BOXES* Small plastic or cardboard boxes for storing labels removed while work is in progress, and for safe keeping of chips and other small pieces of ceramic before they are ready to be bonded.

BOTTLES AND JARS* Bottles should be bought in a variety of shapes and sizes, and save small household jars, some with screw tops, to contain powders. Stoneware marmalade jars make marvellous containers in which brushes will stand upright to dry, and modelling tools and other small implements can be kept within easy reach.

PAPER TOWELS Useful for wiping up spills and for cleaning paint dishes.

ASSORTED BRUSHES Soft painter's brushes, cheap artist's oil painting brushes, small photographer's brush, cheap wooden-backed nail brushes which can be bought at Woolworth's, old toothbrushes and any other useful shapes, for cleaning and dusting purposes.

PALETTES AND MIXING SAUCERS Plain white tiles and off-cuts of plate glass are useful for mixing adhesives and mixing batches of glaze medium with colours. Porcelain mixing saucers also used for mixing glaze medium.

ABRASIVE OR SANDPAPERS* Sandpapers in several grades, from very fine to medium, are for sanding composition fillings, and painted surfaces between each layer. Flexigrit A400 abrasive film is excellent for sanding painted surfaces.

RESPIRATOR* Duralair respirator (Eastern Safety Equipment Respirators) with replaceable *mist* filters to protect from solvent fumes.

GOGGLES* Goggles with flexible mask, which can be worn with the respirator. Protect the eyes if doing much spraying.

DISPOSABLE GLOVES* To protect hands against solvents.

BARRIER CREAMS* Use to protect hands when doing very dirty jobs.

CLEANSING CREAMS* Will remove dirt from hands.

PROTECTIVE CLOTHING* Overalls and aprons.

SAND BOX* Box filled with sand to hold bonded pieces.

MAGNIFYING GLASS* Folding pocket magnifier, X10.

VOLATILE CRAYONS* (CHINA MARKING PENCILS).
TRACING PAPER*.
CELLULOID Used when burnishing gold leaf.

4. Materials

The materials used in the conservation and repair of pottery and porcelain have for many years been the subject of controversy. With advances in the general area of conservation, and modern testing methods, the field has been narrowed to a small number of products which are used in the conservation laboratories of the major museums, and can thus be considered reliable.

Some restorers are inclined to use the latest materials straight from the shop without testing them themselves or asking the advice of the experts. It is for this reason that the new atmosphere of co-operation between conservation departments and professional restorers, as well as the amateur, is so welcome.

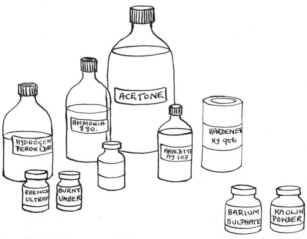

Fig. 2. Labels are very important

The 'perfect' adhesive or the 'perfect' glaze medium has yet to be discovered. As in Chapter 3 the materials marked * are essential.

BOTTLES AND JARS All bottles and jars should be clearly labelled and, especially if there are children in the house, stored in a locked metal cabinet. Use a measure to transfer the contents to the mixing palette or paint dish. Pouring straight from the bottle *can* result in disaster!

Adhesives

ABLEBOND 342-1 EPOXY RESIN, PARTS A AND B* Three parts A to one part B by weight. Warm to 110°F. Crystallization in A is normal. Better colour than Araldite AY 103 and easier to use.

ARALDITE TWO-TUBE PACK (DEVCON '2-TON')* Strong epoxy resin adhesive, for bonding all kitchen wares and for mixing with fillers to form compositions. Use methylated spirits (alcohol) as the solvent.

ARALDITE AY 103 AND HARDENER HY 956* Epoxy resin adhesive for bonding porcelain, except kitchen wares (it will not withstand detergents and immersion in hot water). Like the Two-Tube Araldite, it has a tendency to yellow but to a lesser degree. Titanium dioxide can be added to counteract this and also to give a little more 'body' to the adhesive as well as to give a better match with white porcelain. It is mixed with fillers to make a useful composition for building up and modelling, and for filling moulds. Use methylated spirits (alcohol) to work the composition and for cleaning tools and palette.

POLYVINYL ACETATE EMULSION (P.V.A.) VINAMUL 6815 (C M BOND M-3)* For bonding pottery and stoneware and for mixing with plaster of Paris and powder colours to fill in cracks and build up pottery. Marble flour (marble powder) or fine sand can be added to give a gritty texture when building up large areas. Soluble in acetone, but the surface of a filled-in area can be smoothed with a modelling tool dipped in water.

CYANOACRYLATE RESIN LOCTITE I.S. 496 (ARON ALPHA)* This adhesive, which sets almost instantaneously, can be useful for some porcelain repair, but cannot be used with fillers. Solvent: acetone. **Caution:** extreme care must be taken when using cyanoacrylate. Keep a container of acetone close at hand. If any of the adhesive touches skin, remove it *immediately* with acetone. If fingers should become bonded together, *immerse in acetone. Do not pull apart while dry*. After a few minutes in the solvent they will part without harm to skin. Take care also not to bond fingers or tools to the porcelain.

POLYESTER RESIN, SINTOLIT TRANSPARENT Strong adhesive for pottery and stoneware; do not use on porcelain. Apply sparingly to centre of join. Work with alcohol. Use mask and goggles. Discolours.

Fillers

Fillers are powders which, when mixed with an adhesive, form compositions for filling in, building up and modelling.

TITANIUM DIOXIDE POWDER* A fine white pigment. Add to either Two-Tube Araldite, or Araldite AY 103 (Devcon '2-ton', or Epotek 301 or R.P. 103) to lessen the tendency to yellowing, and to form compositions, usually in conjunction with one of the other filling powders mentioned below, and dry powder pigments. Store in an airtight jar.

BARYTES POWDER (BARIUM SULPHATE)* An inert powder used with titanium dioxide to make compositions for cracks and chips and with other fillers to build up porcelain.

KAOLIN POWDER* An inert powder used with titanium dioxide and other fillers to make compositions for filling in and building up porcelain. Dries a very pale honey colour if used without titanium dioxide.

PLASTER OF PARIS, DENTAL QUALITY (SNOW WHITE NO. 1)* Used with polyvinyl acetate emulsion to make pottery fillings. This combination is not suitable for porcelain because the resulting composition is not strong enough. Store in a dry place.

MARBLE FLOUR (MARBLE POWDER)* Mix with either of the Araldite (Devcon '2-ton', Epotek 301 or R.P. 103) adhesives plus titanium dioxide, if a very strong composition is required for hard-paste porcelain, or with polyvinyl acetate emulsion and plaster of Paris for stoneware. The resultant filling will be very hard, and granular in texture. Store in a dry place.

POLYFILLA A cellulose filling material which needs only the addition of water to form a thick paste, and is used for filling in and building up pottery. Powder colours are also added to match the filling to the pottery, and marble flour or fine sand can be added for texture.

FINE SURFACE POLYFILLA Comes ready-mixed in plastic containers and needs only the addition of powder colours.

Materials for cleaning and preparation

DISTILLED WATER* For all washing operations, unless the restorer owns a de-ionizing (demineralizing) unit.

ACETONE* For dissolving cellulose adhesives, removing old repairs by soaking, removing previously applied paints and varnishes, cleaning edges before bonding. Highly inflammable. Drying to the skin. Unpleasant vapour. Label carefully.

AMMONIA 880 (AMMONIA 28 %)* Used with distilled or de-ionized (demineralized) water to wash porcelain. A few drops are added to hydrogen peroxide and water when bleaching porcelain. It can also be used to remove green marks left by copper or brass rivets.

INDUSTRIAL METHYLATED SPIRITS (DENATURED ETHYL ALCOHOL)* In the UK, a *licence* to use must be obtained from H.M. Customs. Mixed with ammonia in a 50 per cent solution for breaking down shellac. Used when bonding with all types of epoxy resin adhesive, to clean tools and palette and to remove excess adhesive. Can also be used to smooth the surface of epoxy resin adhesive-based compositions when filling in and building up. Inflammable. Unpleasant vapour. Label carefully. Do not drink!

HYDROGEN PEROXIDE, 100 VOL (HYDROGEN PEROXIDE 30–35 %)* Used for bleaching discoloured areas and stained cracks: one part hydrogen peroxide to three parts water, and a few drops of ammonia.[4] **Caution:** poisonous, very harmful to the skin, wash hands immediately in cold water if they come in contact with the peroxide. Ruinous to clothes and fabrics.

[4] See J. Larney, Studies in Conservation, 16 (1971), 69–82, page 71.

DETERGENT: SYNPERONIC NDB (TRITON X100)* A non-ionic surface agent used for washing. Use approximately 1 per cent with water.

NITROMORS (METHYLENE CHLORIDE)* Water-washable paint remover. For removing old paint, varnish and epoxy resins. Will also dissolve rubber cement-type adhesives, and even shellac. Keep well away from varnished furniture. If it touches the skin, wash in cold water immediately.

FERROCLENE 389 (NAVAL JELLY)* Basically phosphoric acid, apply to rust marks left by iron rivets, and some other stains.

SEPIOLITE (MAGNESIUM TRISILICATE)* For removing stains from pottery, which must first be soaked in water. Mix Sepiolite with water to a thick paste and apply to the stained area. Leave for about twenty-four hours, when the Sepiolite will have dried out and have drawn the stain out of the ceramic.

WHITE SPIRIT (STODDARD SOLVENT) Use as turpentine. It is milder than turpentine. Will sometimes dissolve rubber cement. Unpleasant vapour.

Modelling and moulding materials

PLASTICINE (ROMA PLASTELINA ITALIAN NO. 2 WHITE)* For taking simple impressions, for simple moulds on rims of plates, cups, etc. Also used to support bonded objects.

MODELLING WAX* For making models from which casts are to be taken. Keep cool while working. Can be put in refrigerator to harden. Dust with talc before taking a cast.

RUBBER LATEX MOULDS* Rubber latex moulds can be used for hands and arms, handles, flowers and almost every type of moulding operation that may confront the restorer. For very small moulds, three or four layers are painted on, allowing the latex to dry between each layer. For larger moulds it will be necessary to strengthen the latex by adding very small snippets of cotton wool, butter-muslin or cheese-cloth. If it is necessary to strengthen the mould further, a plaster of Paris support or 'mother' has to be added to the outside of the latex mould. The inside of the mould must be dusted with talc or French chalk, before the composition is put into the mould. Latex rubber moulds can be re-used if they have not stretched. Fit back onto the pattern and make a second plaster 'mother'.

SILICONE RUBBER MOULDS* Silicone rubber moulds, which come with their own curing agents, are good for areas where a rigid mould is required. Being rather inflexible when cured they are not as versatile in their uses as the rubber latex moulds. Useful for areas of surface moulding. Use mixing ratios given with individual brands. *Some silicone rubber moulds must be cured in the oven at 59°C (150°F) for one hour before filling with the composition, see individual instructions.*

DENTAL IMPRESSION COMPOUND PARIBAR (MERCAPTAN-MIM)* Useful for simple impressions.

Glaze mediums and their solvents, paints and pigments

CHINAGLAZE CLEAR GLOSS Two-pack urea formaldehyde/melamine formaldehyde lacquer. Cold-setting (unless used without catalyst). Use with Phenthin 83, solvent and brush cleaner.

BEDACRYL 122X (ACRYLOID B48N) An air-drying surface coating used as a glaze medium, which is water white but requires great skill if used on porcelain. Good for pottery. *Cellosolve* (acetate) solvent must be added to give better flow, approximately 50 per cent to 50 per cent of the thinner, which is *Xylene*. (The proportions are not critical.)

CHINTEX* An oven-drying glaze medium which must be baked at 94°C (220°F). Comes with its *own thinner and brush cleaner*.* (In U.S. use high aromatic or keytone automotive lacquer thinner.)

MATTING AGENT GASIL 23C (CABOSIL)* Incorporated into whichever glaze medium is being used, to achieve a matt surface for Parian ware, Wedgwood, and unglazed pottery.

DRY POWDER PIGMENT* Colours in powder form. Buy artist's quality only. The following list of pigments should be sufficient for the restorer's needs but each artist will find others to add to them. They must be very thoroughly mixed, whether for use with compositions or glaze mediums. *Colours :* titanium white, ivory black, French ultramarine blue, cobalt blue, cerulean blue, viridian green, burnt sienna, cadmium red, light red, alizarin crimson, burnt umber, raw umber, aureolin yellow, Winsor lemon, yellow ochre, raw sienna.

ARTIST'S OIL COLOURS* The oil content of these colours makes them less suitable for mixing with glaze mediums than the powder pigments. However, by squeezing them onto a piece of thick white paper a great deal of the oil can be drained off. This should be done as much as twenty-four hours before use. Their one advantage over powder pigments is that they do not produce a granular surface. *Colours :* titanium white, ivory black, Payne's grey, ultramarine blue, cerulean blue, viridian green, burnt sienna, cadmium red, alizarin crimson, rose madder genuine, light red, Indian red, burnt umber, raw umber, Winsor lemon, aurora yellow, yellow ochre, Naples yellow, raw sienna.

ARTIST'S ACRYLIC COLOURS For use on pottery only. *Not* suitable for objects in use.

MAIMERI COLOURS New, totally oilfree paints from Italy. Thin with white spirit (Stoddard Solvent). Use over plaster. Use with Acryloid B48N and Cabosil matting agent on pottery.

Gilding

TRANSFER GOLD LEAF* Gold leaf comes in a small booklet, interleaved with acid-free tissue paper. It is sold in several colours; the 24 carat, the 23½ carat, and the white gold will cover the restorer's requirements. It also comes in several other colours but the occasions on which these would be required are so rare that the expense is not justified. The white gold leaf can also be used for silver decoration.

TABLET GOLD Gold powder, bound with gum arabic, and sold in the form of a minute tablet. Very expensive!

BRONZE POWDERS* These are included despite their short-comings. It is very difficult to obtain a smooth, gilded look with these powders and they tend to discolour with age. Mixed thoroughly with whichever glaze medium is being used for the object, the discoloration can be retarded. For best results gold leaf is recommended. Buy only the best quality bronze powders, very finely ground. The most useful colours are: rich pale gold lining, English burnishing bronzes Nos. 1, 3 and 10.

Surface finishing

SIMONIZ CAR POLISH A little of this polish applied on a damp rag with a very gentle circular motion, will reduce the gloss on a finished glaze surface, so long as the glaze is *absolutely* dry. Great care must be taken not to disturb the surface of the glaze.

SOLVOL AUTOSOL* A chromium polish which will also bring up the gloss on a glazed surface. Use *sparingly* on a dry cloth.

RENAISSANCE WAX* A very fine-textured wax polish which is sometimes useful for improving the surface of a glaze.

Miscellaneous materials

TALC For dusting out latex and silicone rubber moulds.

SLIPWAX RELEASE AGENT (NON-SILICONE) (BUTCHER'S WAX)* Used to prevent rubber moulds sticking to plaster of Paris support and silicone rubber mould sections sticking to each other. Avoid contact with inside surface of moulds.

Notes: Polyvinyl Alcohol Resin mixed with water painted inside moulds makes an excellent release agent, as an alternative to talc.

The matting agent Gasil 23C (Cabosil) can also be used to stiffen epoxy fillings and prevent them from collapsing.

(Attapulgus Clay 200 Mesh provides a good alternative to Magnesium Trisilicate.)

(See special instructions included with Snow White Plaster No. 1, page 30.)

5. Protection while working

Protective clothing

By devoting a separate section to the discussion of protective wear, it is possible to stress its importance. Spilt solvents and adhesives ruin clothes, so it is recommended that an overall and a tough carpenter's apron be worn. The latter also serves to bridge the gap between the knees and can thus save many a small piece from falling to the floor and becoming lost or broken.

Skin protection

The hands will come into contact with solvents and adhesives which are harmful to the skin. The use of barrier creams is one form of protection and fine disposable gloves can be used for many jobs. Ordinary kitchen rubber gloves are not recommended because they are too thick for the handling of fragile objects.

Respirator and goggles

Unless the ventilation is so efficient that the fumes are removed as they occur, it is strongly recommended that a simple respirator be worn when using the airbrush. Goggles provide protection for the eyes when spraying, and if irritation is felt when using some adhesives, particularly cyanoacrylates. The important thing is to be aware of possible harmful effects of the materials and to have the deterrents at hand.

In the materials list will be found all the solvents mentioned in the text. The appropriate solvent *for use while work is in progress* is given with each adhesive in Chapter 4. The solvents for *removing* adhesives when found in old repairs are given in Chapter 7: 'Cleaning and preparation'.

6. Choosing the first project

An exciting moment has arrived—the aspiring restorer must decide which piece of pottery or porcelain to choose for his first efforts at repairing. How can he decide which would be the most suitable? Bonding is the first step and obviously it would be foolhardy to start with a large piece with multiple breaks. Start looking in the kitchen where items of lesser value are to be found, such as plates in two or three pieces, a teapot lid missing its knob, or a cup with its handle lying forlornly beside it. After bonding, most pieces will have to have cracks and chips filled in and many of them will have larger sections missing which will need building up. Once the missing parts have been filled in or built up they must be disguised by painting, or retouching, and sometimes gilding. For very extensive repairs, moulds will have to be taken from patterns and casts taken from the moulds.

Some pieces will need reinforcing with dowels, and there will be hands to build up by direct modelling, from a photograph or from memory. Bearing these stages in mind, a suitable object can be chosen or purchased. Many antique dealers are glad to sell their damaged porcelain and pottery at reasonable prices rather than send it to a restorer and have to wait months for its return. It is worth while making friends with a knowledgeable dealer who will usually be happy to give information and help to someone who shows genuine interest.

The choice will depend on the type of wares collected, but it is worth bearing in mind that pottery and soft-paste porcelain are easier to repair than hard-paste porcelain. Lustre ware and heavily gilded pieces should be avoided by the beginner because they are both extremely difficult to restore. The application of the gold leaf and attempting to match lustre can be very depressing to one with no experience. Staffordshire groups are amusing to work on and can be rewarding because good results are usually achieved. Any piece that will involve painting large areas of ground colour should be avoided because, again, this is arduous and somewhat depressing work for the beginner.

7. Cleaning and preparation

Cleaning is the very important first stage in repairing pottery and porcelain. Pieces that have been repaired previously must be completely free of all traces of old adhesives and paint before any new work can be started. Newly broken porcelain must be swabbed with acetone to remove any greasy fingermarks or specks of dust which might prevent good bonding. Very dusty porcelain can be washed in warm water and ammonia, using a soft brush. Rinse in clear water. Drain on a lint-free cloth and leave in a warm place to dry completely. Do not bond damp porcelain because the adhesive will not set satisfactorily.

EPOXY RESIN ADHESIVE ON PORCELAIN: NITROMORS (METHYLENE CHLORIDE) Inspect the piece to be repaired very carefully, with a magnifying glass if necessary, to find out where the old breaks are, and what kind of adhesive was used. To break down epoxy resin joins, paint them with Nitromors (methylene chloride) paint stripper and leave to soften for about an hour in a covered container. It may take several applications before all the adhesive has softened sufficiently to permit separation of the joins. Once the pieces have been separated, use Nitromors (methylene chloride) to clean the edges. A scalpel blade can be used *very* gently to lift the softened epoxy, but take great care not to damage the porcelain. Swab off the Nitromors (methylene chloride) with water between each coating.

EPOXY RESIN ADHESIVES ON POTTERY: NITROMORS (METHYLENE CHLORIDE) The only difference in removing epoxy resin adhesives from pottery is that, to prevent the Nitromors (methylene chloride) and the dissolving adhesives from being drawn into the porous body of the piece, the edges must be swabbed with water before the application of the Nitromors (methylene chloride). This is done by dipping a brush in water and dabbing it onto the edges, or by laying swabs of wet cotton wool along the edges, making sure that it soaks in well. Then apply the Nitromors (methylene chloride) and leave in a covered container for about an hour, swabbing off the edges and renewing the application as often as required. Again, it may be necessary to lift some of the old adhesive away from the breaks with a scalpel blade, using extreme care.

SHELLAC ON POTTERY AND PORCELAIN: INDUSTRIAL METHY-LATED SPIRITS AND AMMONIA 880, OR NITROMORS (ETHYL ALCOHOL AND AMMONIA 28%, OR METHYLENE CHLORIDE) Shellac, which looks like toffee, is difficult to remove, especially if it has been burnt on. (Shellac is applied by heating both the ceramic and the shellac.) With porcelain, try soaking in very hot, *not* boiling, water, and then use a scalpel blade to lift it gently away from the porcelain. Industrial methylated spirits (ethyl alcohol) mixed with ammonia 880 (ammonia 28%) in a 50 per cent solution, can be used to break down shellac, and sometimes Nitromors (methylene chloride) will remove it. Do not use household methylated spirits because it is dyed to distinguish it from other liquids and the dye can leave a stain impossible to remove, especially on pottery and soft-paste porcelain. With pottery, a second hazard to be avoided is that of either the solvent or the old adhesive being drawn into the ceramic. To avoid this, pre-soak the object in water, either distilled or de-ionized, then coat the piece with Nitromors (methylene chloride) and leave in a covered container. Re-soak the piece in water after swabbing off the first application and repeat until the edges are clean.

ANIMAL GLUES: HOT WATER These are usually pale brown, have a distinctive odour and are dissolved in hot, *not boiling*, water, using a soft brush very gently to clean the edges.

RUBBER CEMENT: NITROMORS (METHYLENE CHLORIDE) OR WHITE SPIRIT The adhesives known as rubber cements are very similar to rubber in texture and, in the case of porcelain, can usually be pulled off by hand, leaving the edges free to be thoroughly cleaned with Nitromors (methylene chloride). With pottery, do not pull off the rubber cement because it may loosen some of the pottery, which will break away, causing unnecessary damage. Nitromors (methylene chloride) or White Spirit will dissolve rubber cement, but remember to wet edges when using Nitromors (methylene chloride) on pottery.

CELLULOSE ADHESIVES: ACETONE The clear adhesives, known as cellulose adhesives, are easily dissolved in acetone. When soaking an object in acetone, always use a covered container because this solvent evaporates very quickly. Lay figures on their sides or wrap them in butter-muslin or cheese-cloth to prevent arms or other loose pieces from falling off and breaking when the adhesive dissolves. For large pieces, use a plastic kitchen bowl covered with foil tucked under the edge of the bowl.

Remember, most solvents will damage furniture, so take the utmost care to keep them from splashing and use only on the Formica surface, on a plain wood surface, or in a plastic bowl.

After cleaning, inspect all edges with a magnifying glass to make certain that *all* traces of old adhesive have been removed. Sometimes it will be necessary to coax out the minutest pieces with the tip of a blade, again using great care. Give a final swab with acetone.

OLD PAINTS AND VARNISHES: NITROMORS (METHYLENE CHLORIDE) OR ACETONE With pottery, again damp the surrounding areas with water to prevent absorption of the Nitromors (methylene chloride) or the paint into the pottery.

STAINS A very useful recipe for the removal of stains and ingrained dirt is the one used at the Victoria and Albert Museum.[5] Mix one part hydrogen peroxide 100 vol. (hydrogen peroxide 30–35%) with three parts water and add a few drops of ammonia. Dip pieces of cotton wool in this solution and lay on the surface of the glaze over the stained area, or directly onto broken edges which are discoloured. Put in a covered container or wrap in clear plastic. Repeat until stain has disappeared, then wash in distilled or de-ionized water. Again, pottery needs different treatment from porcelain. Soak pottery in water

[5] See J. Larney, 'Studies in Conservation', 16 (1970), 69–82, page 71.

before applying the swabs to prevent the stain spreading to other areas of the piece. Leave the swabs in place for not more than two hours. Change them as often as necessary, remembering to *re-soak pottery* in water before each application.

This method has been used with particular success on a very badly stained Creamware jug which had a dark, greasy patch of many years' standing. The grease had penetrated through the pottery from the inside to the outside. Swabs were laid on both surfaces, covered with plastic and changed constantly over a period of two weeks. The resulting disappearance of the stain was miraculous. A section of transfer printing which had been almost invisible, became clearly defined. Swabbing the area with acetone between each application of hydrogen peroxide solution will sometimes help to remove some of the stain, and will also dry out the area, thus making it possible to see how much of the stain is left.

Caution: Always wear gloves while handling hydrogen peroxide solution—it is harmful to the skin and to fabrics. Should any of the mixture be spilt on the hands, wash it off immediately with cold water. Fabrics will be permanently damaged so take extra precautions to protect clothing.

REMOVAL OF RIVETS (CLAMPS) Another problem which the restorer will have to face is the removal of rivets (clamps). Rivets are small metal clamps used to join sections of broken

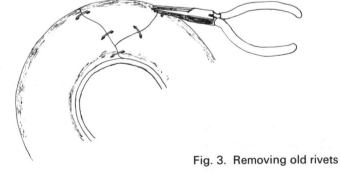

Fig. 3. Removing old rivets

porcelain and pottery. Before the advent of epoxy resins, they were used a great deal for all types of joins, but are now reserved mainly for heavy plates and dishes in everyday use. They are unsightly and should *never* be used on valuable objects.

Before attempting to remove rivets (clamps), soak in hot (not boiling) water, which will loosen the plaster of Paris with which the holes at both ends of each rivet (clamp) are filled. Remove as much of the plaster as can be reached with a dental tool. With a pair of pliers, try to lift the rivet (clamp) very gently, one end at a time, pulling up and away from the length of the rivet (clamp). If this does not work, it will be necessary to saw through the rivet (clamp) with the *blade* of a hacksaw. Extreme care must be taken not to touch the glaze with the blade. Hold the rivet with the thumb to prevent it from rocking to and fro and possibly causing a chip of porcelain to break away from one of the holes. Having sawn the rivet in half, gently lever out each piece of rivet (clamp) with the pliers, again taking care not to chip the ceramic. Some plaster will remain in the holes and this can be scraped out with a dental probe. Wash the piece thoroughly in water, or swab with acetone.

OTHER STAINS Rivets (clamps) very often leave stains. Rust marks left by iron rivets (clamps) can be removed, or lessened, by the application of a product called Ferroclene (Naval Jelly), which is basically phosphoric acid. After use rinse the piece several times in distilled or de-ionized water. Try ammonia 880 (ammonia 28%) or the hydrogen peroxide recipe (see pages 31 and 41) for cleaning off green marks left by copper or brass rivets (clamps).

WASHING SYNPERONIC N.D.B. (TRITON X100) is a safe detergent for washing ceramics but should be used sparingly, approximately 1 per cent with water.

LABELS Labels are often found on ceramics and, in most cases, are of importance. If the object needs cleaning by soaking, the labels must be removed with care and kept until the work has been completed. If there is ink on the label, test it in one spot to see if it is soluble in water. If not, the label may be soaked off. If the ink appears to run, it will have to be removed very carefully with a blade. Sometimes a little water can be pushed under the edges of the label with the tip of a clean paint brush and this will facilitate removal.

8. Putting the pieces together

Bonding is the term used to describe the joining of broken pottery and porcelain. It requires skill and patience and, like all the processes in restoration, is mastered in time and with practice. Accuracy is essential because even the smallest degree of inaccuracy in building up a multiple break will result in an uneven surface and a crooked object. *Filling in and painting will not disguise a badly reconstructed piece of ceramic.* The restorer should be highly critical of his work at each stage and should re-bond a piece which is out of position.

Two-Tube Araldite (Devcon '2-ton') can be used for all kitchen wares because it is very strong and will withstand a considerable amount of washing in hot water with detergents. It can also be combined with various fillers to make compositions for building up missing pieces and filling chips. Two-Tube Araldite (Devcon '2-ton') is, unfortunately, a deep yellow when mixed, so it is seldom possible to produce an invisible join with this adhesive, which, moreover, darkens with age. To counteract this tendency, a small amount of titanium dioxide powder can be added. To use Araldite (Devcon '2-ton') successfully, spread the thinnest smear *onto one edge only*, with the boxwood modelling tool. *Gentle* heat will enable a closer join to be achieved.

Assemble the tools and materials before starting to bond. Once the adhesive has been applied there is no time to hunt for tape with which to hold the section together! Adhesive, industrial methylated spirits (ethyl alcohol), titanium dioxide, powder colours, boxwood modelling tool, metal spatula, white tile or piece of plate glass, a clean rag, pair of fine, pointed tweezers, Scotch tape, clean paint brush and finally, a pair of *very* clean hands!

To get the feel of handling porcelain without fear of damaging a valuable object, start with kitchen ware—a plate in two pieces. Having cleaned it, following instructions in the last chapter, give the edges a final wipe with acetone to remove fingermarks, and inspect for dust particles. Before applying adhesive bring the edges together very gently and notice the 'sensation' when they meet. This is important because it will help in achieving a good join without too much movement of the pieces once the adhesive is in place. Get into the habit of fitting the pieces together in this way before each bonding job. Do not grate the edges together— this could break off minute fragments and spoil the look of the join. (If this should happen, brush the edges lightly with a soft bristle brush.)

How to use : Mix equal portions from each tube of Two-Tube Araldite (Devcon '2-ton') on a palette, using a boxwood modelling tool, or a metal spatula. When thoroughly blended clean the tool with methylated spirits (ethyl alcohol). A little titanium dioxide powder can be added to lighten the adhesive, or a very little powder colour can be used to make the mixture blend in with coloured ceramic. Keep the colour on the light side. Sit back in a comfortable position with the back supported. Take the larger section of the plate in the left hand and spread a *thin film* of Two-Tube Araldite (Devcon '2-ton') along *one* edge. Remember, the less adhesive, the better the bond. The beginner always tends to use too much. Take the other section in the right hand and slowly bring the two edges together so that they meet horizontally, remembering just how they 'felt' when they were keyed without adhesive. With experience it will be possible to know at once whether the pieces are correctly aligned, but at first it may be difficult to tell. An almost imperceptible rocking movement will sometimes settle the piece into position. Do not press the pieces together firmly until they are aligned, because small fragments could chip off, and, becoming mixed with the adhesive, necessitate a fresh start.

One way to test the accuracy of the join is to run a fingernail

1. A cabbage-shaped pot before bonding

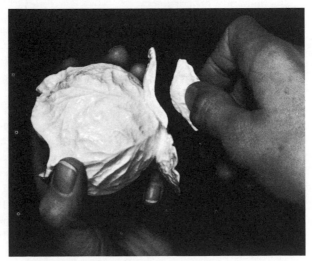

2. Adding the second piece

3. The finger test for accuracy

gently up and down across the join (the join is still horizontal).
If the nail catches on either edge, the bond is inaccurate. If it
catches on the *upper edge* the *upper* piece of porcelain needs to
be very gently moved *outwards* to bring it into position on the
lower piece. If the nail catches on the *lower* section, move the
upper piece slowly inwards, keeping the lower half in the same
position with the left hand. After manoeuvring the pieces to
form a good key, then, and only then, is the time to apply firm
pressure so that the excess adhesive exudes from the join,
leaving only the amount necessary to set into a firm bond. Keep
the fingers away from the break—it is amazing how quickly a
join can become dirty. The plate can now be stood in the sand
box, with the join running horizontally, and left undisturbed
for five or six hours to harden. This will be assisted by a warm
atmosphere. If a sand box is not available the plate can be stood
in a box containing well-crushed paper, or wedged in a large

pad of Plasticine (Roma Plastelina). Neither of these is as satisfactory as the sand box.

A simple two-piece bond which is well balanced can be put in the sand box without strapping. However, most joins *will* need to be strapped. This is done with Scotch tape which is cut into lengths of 5–8 cm (2–3 in). (For very large or very small objects, increase or decrease the length.) Attach the strips to the *upper* section of the plate at right angles to the join, and pull them gently down onto the lower section. For a dinner plate five pieces placed at equal distances should be sufficient. Repeat on the other side. The plate can be held with the left hand and the tape applied by the right hand, using a featherlight touch. Alternatively, stand the lower section of the plate in the sand box *before* bonding, apply the adhesive and place the upper section in position, making certain that the join is exactly horizontal. Attach the Scotch tape and leave to set. If much adhesive has squeezed out it should be gently removed with a clean paint brush dipped in methylated spirits (ethyl alcohol). Shake off the excess and push the tip of the brush gently under the adhesive, when it will lift off quite easily. Do not flood the join because the methylated spirits (ethyl alcohol) will dilute the Araldite (Devcon '2-ton') and weaken the bond.

The sprung or warped join After practising on several plates, try another exercise in bonding. Still using Two-Tube Araldite (Devcon '2-ton') choose something completely different, say a cup, with a piece broken out of the rim. The cup will be much easier to hold than the plate, but the piece may be more difficult to fit into place. Holding the larger section of the cup in the left hand, fit the chip into the gap to see how it meets the other edge. If the porcelain is fairly thick it will probably fit well, but with fine porcelain a piece out of the rim can often be 'warped' or 'sprung'. This means that one end of the piece will not lie smoothly against the body of the cup. To counteract this, *apply adhesive to one half of the gap only*, fit the piece into place and make sure that the join is accurate as far as the adhesive reaches. Strap with Scotch tape, and, starting on the inside

Fig. 4. The sprung break—one side is bonded and taped and allowed to dry before bonding the second half

bring the tape up and over the rim of the cup, including the section without adhesive, and smooth it down onto the outside. Stand the cup aside to set overnight. Since the join is horizontal when the cup is upright, there is no need to put it in the sand box. Next, gently press more Araldite (Devcon '2-ton') between the cup edge and the remaining part of the piece, warming the cup if necessary. Attach some Scotch tape to the inside of the cup. With the left hand slowly coax the sprung piece into position and bring the tape up over the rim of the cup with the right hand, using it to continue putting pressure on the sprung piece. Do not use force or the piece may break. Keep on practising simple joins until it no longer seems difficult, then try multiple breaks.

Multiple breaks The secret with multiple breaks is to make a 'trial run' before applying the adhesive, thereby avoiding the frustrating experience of 'locking out' a piece, and having to undo the work already completed. This can be done either by fitting the pieces together and remembering their sequence, or by rebuilding the object, using Scotch tape to hold it in shape and numbering each piece. The numbers are written on tiny pieces of brown adhesive packing tape attached to the ceramic, but kept away from the joins. When the numbering has been

4. A Chinese Export plate in six pieces

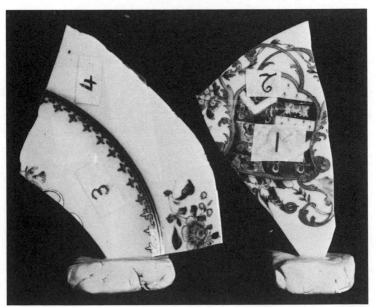

5. The first four pieces bonded, strapped and propped

6. This will be the final join

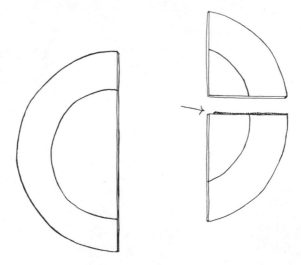

Fig. 5. Apply adhesive to within $\frac{1}{8}$ in of end of first join. This will prevent dried adhesive from obstructing the fit in the second join

completed remove the Scotch tape very carefully, using acetone to avoid stripping off gold leaf with the tape. To assemble, it is usually best to start with the largest piece and build from there. Sometimes it is more satisfactory to put two smaller pieces together when they will fit into a wide angle, rather than adding them one at a time. When bonding a multiple break apply the adhesive to within 0·31 cm ($\frac{1}{8}$ in) of the end of the join if a second join is to cross it at right angles. Adhesive exuding from the end of a join which has been allowed to dry, will obstruct a second join. Handles can safely be bonded with Two-Tube Araldite (Devcon '2-ton') if the piece is not for daily use. A handle which must withstand the weight of a teacup full of hot liquid, or a jug full of milk, should be dowelled. Dowelling instructions will be found in Chapter 9. Cups, and other objects with handles, which are only decorative, are unlikely to be lifted by their handles, so bonding with Araldite (Devcon '2-ton') will be perfectly satisfactory. If the handle is in several pieces, reconstruct it before bonding it to the object. It is seldom possible to strap the sections of a handle, so they will have to be propped in a small pad of Plasticine (Roma Plastelina) with the join running horizontally and the upper piece perfectly balanced. Find the balance *before* applying the adhesive. When the handle is ready to be bonded to the cup, place two strips of Scotch tape on the inside of the cup, positioned diagonally, 3·75 cm ($1\frac{1}{2}$ in) to 5 cm (2 in). (This will of course depend on the size of the cup.) Once the handle is in place bring one of the strips up, out, and across the handle and press it down onto the cup. Do the same with the other piece of tape, pulling it in the other direction and crossing the first piece about half way down the handle. To form a good bond with the cup the handle must be accurately assembled and carefully bonded to the cup. Place the cup in the sand box or wedge with a pad of Plasticine (Roma Plastelina), with the handle in the horizontal position. When the adhesive is dry some cleaning may be necessary. Using a double-edged razor blade, gently lift the dry adhesive away from the porcelain, taking the greatest care not to scratch the glaze. The adhesive can be softened with methylated spirits (ethyl alcohol) if it is very hard. Make sure that there is no dried adhesive elsewhere on the surface of the glaze.

Araldite AY 103 with Hardener HY 956 and Ablebond 342-1 epoxy resin, parts A and B are used for porcelain which is not in daily use and also mixed with powders to form compositions for filling chips and cracks and building up missing pieces. This composition is used too for filling moulds, and for modelling. There is another hardener, HY 951, sold for use with Araldite AY 103 but it is said to be more harmful to the skin. Care should be taken when handling epoxy resins because some skins are allergic to them.

Araldite AY 103 and Ablebond 342-1 are less viscous than Two-Tube Araldite (Devcon '2-ton') and the mixing is more critical: five parts of AY 103 to one part HY 956, three parts Ablebond 342-1 to one part hardener by weight. Use either a small kitchen spoon or a metal rod from which drops can be dripped into a container. Weigh on gramme scales to ensure accuracy. Measure into a small paper container made with greaseproof or waxed paper, remembering to make allowance for its weight. Araldite AY 103 has a tendency to yellow but not as badly as Two-Tube Araldite (Devcon '2-ton'). It too can be lightened with titanium dioxide powder. Ablebond 342–1 has, to date, the least tendency to yellowing. Weigh accurately, after warming to 110°F, then use as Araldite AY 103.

How to use: Araldite AY 103, HY 956 and Ablebond 342-1 epoxy resin, parts A and B are used for bonding antique porcelain. The proportions *must* be accurate—5 parts of Araldite AY 103 to one part HY 956, 3 parts Ablebond 342-1 epoxy resin A to one part B—to ensure a successful bond. The simplest way to measure this adhesive in small quantities is to use the smallest kitchen measuring spoon. Alternatively a metal rod can be used, dipping the rod into the adhesive and transferring it to the container, then cleaning the rod before dipping into the hardener. Be sure to mix the adhesive and hardener *very* thoroughly. The mixture will be easier to handle if left partially to set for about one hour, stirring it occasionally. Add a little titanium dioxide powder to counteract the tendency to yellowing. The bonding procedure is the same as for Two-Tube Araldite (Devcon '2-ton') but porcelain is harder to handle with the more liquid adhesive. It has a tendency to slip out of position when a good join has just been achieved. Standing the main section in the sand box before applying the adhesive will avoid movement once the upper piece is in place, and attaching the tape on the upper section, ready for pulling into place, will also avoid too much movement. This adhesive is best left undisturbed for twenty-four hours or more because it takes longer to dry than the Two-Tube (Devcon '2-ton') variety.

Cyanoacrylate resin Loctite IS 49 (Aron Alpha) Cyanoacrylates have only limited uses for the restorer, and are not recommended for valuable pieces. They *cannot* be used for pottery and when used for porcelain the edges to be joined must be *spotlessly* clean, and preferably not previously repaired. They set almost instantly which means that the restorer must work with speed and skill. Some other adhesive should be used for very awkward joins owing to the time limit. A teapot lid, bonded with a cyanoacrylate resin, withstood daily use for a year before breaking down. Cyanoacrylates provide a bond which is invisible except for a hairline. The only way to become adept at bonding is to practise on as many pieces as possible. Friends and relations are usually delighted to provide their least valuable objects for exercises. The cyanoacrylate resins are tricky for a beginner to use because there is no time to manoeuvre the pieces and it is possible to glue the fingers to the porcelain or to each other. It is therefore suggested that cyanoacrylates be used only after considerable experience has been gained with other adhesives.

How to use: Follow these simple precautions: *Read the instructions accompanying the adhesive, keep a container of acetone close at hand, be sure of the fit of the pieces as described earlier (page 46), keep the fingers free of adhesive, and away from the join, use the smallest possible amount of adhesive.* Owing to the almost instant setting no strapping is necessary and this means that a multiple break can be built up into a completed job in a very short time. Should a join be faulty it can be broken down with acetone. Dip a brush in acetone and work it into the join, keeping it away from the ones that are accurate. When sufficiently softened it will be possible to ease the pieces apart and clean them with acetone and a small brush, lifting any obstinate particles with the tip of a scalpel blade.

Cyanoacrylates can be used for everyday porcelain, but remember that they do break down eventually. There is an advantage in using them for multiple breaks with many small pieces because the build-up of adhesive is not sufficient to cause inaccuracy in the final joins, which would produce a lopsided job. This can happen when using a viscous adhesive such as the Two-Tube Araldite (Devcon '2-ton').

Polyvinyl acetate emulsion (P.V.A.), Vinamul 6815 (C M Bond M-3) The texture of polyvinyl acetate emulsion is more suited to pottery than that of epoxy resins; it is colourless when dry and does not cause a problem by seeping under the glaze and creating a stain.

How to use: Progressing to the bonding of pottery with polyvinyl acetate emulsion (P.V.A. for short), a slightly different technique is used. Pottery is much softer than porcelain and is sometimes rather coarse in texture which can give the impression of bonding the two halves of a digestive biscuit. For this reason the edges must not be grated together, or even rocked back and forth to find the exact fit, as was suggested with porcelain. Consolation can be taken from the fact that the key is often easier to find than with porcelain.

As with porcelain the edges to be joined must be free of all dirt and traces of old repairs. The bonding of pottery with P.V.A. is improved by damping both edges with water, using a brush, or laying cotton wool swabs along the edges and leaving for a few minutes. Do not flood the pottery or the adhesive will not bond efficiently. Then apply the adhesive to one edge only,

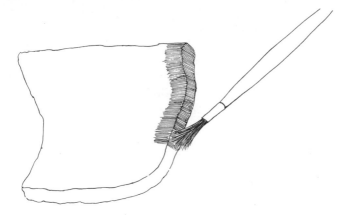

Fig. 6. De-ionized (or distilled) water is applied to pottery before bonding

spreading it on with a spatula or modelling tool, but as with the epoxy resins, do not use more than a thin smear. The damp edges of the pottery will provide a better surface for even dispersal, and prevent the P.V.A. being dried out by having its moisture content absorbed by the dry pottery. The P.V.A. dries clear and is strong enough for the uses for which it is designed. It is water soluble so must not be used for any items that are to be washed. (Inexpensive pottery such as ash trays, mugs, vases, etc. can be bonded with Two-Tube Araldite (Devcon '2-ton') to withstand the rigours of daily use.) The bonded pieces are treated in the same way as the epoxy resin bonds: stood in the sand box, strapped with Scotch tape and left to dry for twenty-four hours.

There are many types and brands of adhesives and the restorer is free to try them for himself, but, to start with, it is recommended that he stay with the four mentioned here. They cover all the restorer's needs and are known to be of good quality. As he learns more about what is required of an adhesive for a given purpose, he will be able to experiment with other brands and types and even manufacture his own. In the list of reference books will be found the title of a publication dealing with every type and brand of adhesive, with addresses of the makers and there are recipes for home-made adhesives. CIBA, the makers of the Araldite adhesives, publish several very interesting pamphlets on their products, including the many and varied uses to which they are put. They are available upon request, and the address will be found in the list of suppliers (page 150).

9. Filling in, building up and reinforcing

Almost every piece of ceramic which has been bonded will require chips, cracks, or missing pieces filling in. Only where there is a new, clean break will it be practicable to put the pieces together and call the job complete. With the exception of museum work, where the restoration is often left free of overpainting or retouching, painting is inevitable.

Simple filling-in exercise The first painting job must be simple, so, in choosing something for the first filling-in exercise, try to find a piece with a chip in a coloured area. Let us suppose that the chip is on the edge of a porcelain plate but does not break the line of the rim, in other words, the filling will not need supporting. Using either the tile or the piece of plate glass as a palette, mix small, equal amounts of Two-Tube Araldite (Devcon '2-ton'), or Araldite AY 103 and Hardener HY 956 or Ablebond 342-1, depending on whether the subject is for use or decoration. (See previous chapter.) Add titanium dioxide powder to whiten the adhesive, and, to make the colour-matching easier, powder pigments can be added now, gradually mixing them with the adhesive to resemble the ceramic, but keeping the filling on the light side.

The restorer will, with experience, decide which combinations of filling materials he prefers. For porcelain, including kitchen wares and decorative wares, add kaolin powder or barytes powder to give body to the filling, and to make it easier to handle. If a filling with a gritty texture is desired, add a little marble flour (marble powder); this will make a strong filling which should not be used on very fine porcelain. The filling mixture should not be so soft that it is too sticky to handle, and, equally it should not be stiff and dry.

Ideally, it should be possible to roll it out like pastry, using one of the filling powders (not marble flour (marble powder)) to prevent it sticking. Apply some thin composition, Araldite or Ablebond 342-1 and titanium dioxide with a little powder pigment, to the inside of the chip. With the tip of the boxwood modelling tool, or the metal spatula, press some of the filling mixture into the chip, pushing it firmly against the sides to expel the air, which may otherwise become trapped and cause pin-holes where it has escaped. Clean the tool in methylated spirits (ethyl alcohol). Now dip it again in the methylated spirits (ethyl alcohol), shake off the excess and gently smooth the surface of the filling. Do not use too much solvent or the mixture will become runny. If there is any mixture on the surface of the surrounding glaze, remove it with a rag dipped in the solvent. Leave the filling until almost set, when it will be possible to smooth the surface level with the glaze, again using the modelling tool and methylated spirits (ethyl alcohol). This will eliminate some of the grinding down and sanding when the filled area is dry.

Filling cracks When filling in cracks a softer mixture should be used, because it will be easier to work in to these confined areas. They are filled by drawing the tip of the tool across the crack and working the mixture into the cavity. Clean the tool and, after dipping in the solvent shake off the excess and smooth the surface of the filling, this time working *along* the crack. Leave until almost hard, then wipe away excess filling. After drying completely, it may be necessary to apply more mixture to small areas that were missed the first time.

Cracks can, after thorough cleaning, be prevented from spreading further by warming the ceramic and running a little adhesive into the crack. Very close cracks should have the adhesive gently worked into them with the boxwood modelling tool.

Fire cracks, those cracks which formed during the original firing of the object, should not be filled. This, however, is a matter of individual opinion.

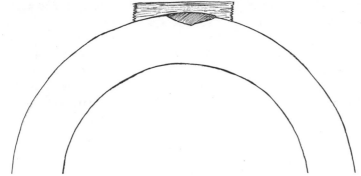

Fig. 7. Scotch tape makes a useful support for small chips

Supports for edge chips Most edge chips *will* require a support for the filling while it is drying. Simple supports can be made for very small chips by stretching Scotch tape across the opening, or a pad of Plasticine (Roma Plastelina) can be pressed against the ceramic. To use tape, cut a piece long enough to overlap the missing section, and stretch it into place. One or two more pieces of tape can be added over the first to give strength. Dust a little talc onto the inside of the tape to separate it from the filling. Press the filling gently into place, remembering to expel the air. Smooth it level with the surface of the china and remove excess filling. Prop the piece so that the filled area is lying horizontally. Plasticine (Roma Plastelina) is useful as a support but it is important to separate it from the filling by dusting with the talc or it will cause a pitted surface. If the damage is in an area where there is a scalloped edge or moulded decoration, a flat piece of Plasticine (Roma Plastelina) will not be of much assistance. Plasticine (Roma Plastelina) can be formed into shaped moulds as follows: roll it out on a flat surface to a thickness of about 1·25 cm ($\frac{1}{2}$ in) and large enough to overlap the missing area. Prop the object in the sand box so that both hands are free, or brace on the knees, using the heel of each palm to steady the plate, freeing the fingers to work the Plasticine (Roma Plastelina). Find a place on the edge of the plate identical with the section to be replaced, damp the china so that the Plasticine (Roma Plastelina) will not stick, and press the pad firmly against the surface, leaving an overlap of about 1·25 cm ($\frac{1}{2}$ in) all round. Lift it carefully away from the object, taking care not to damage the impression. Inspect the mould to make sure that there is a faithful reproduction (in the reverse) of the design. Dust with talc to prevent the filling sticking to the mould. Apply the mould to the break, matching the pattern on either side. Press the overlapping Plasticine (Roma Plastelina) round, but not into, the gap, remembering to avoid touching the impression. Tape can be used to hold it in position. Apply a smear of *thin* Araldite (Devcon '2-ton') or Ablebond 342-1 composition to the edges of the ceramic. Fill the mould with a firm mixture of the composition, pushing it into the corners to expel the air, and smoothing it down to match the edge of the ceramic where it meets the mould. Do not press so hard that the mould is dislodged. Set aside for twenty-four hours. Remove the Plasticine (Roma Plastelina) and clean round the filling with methylated spirits (ethyl alcohol). Sand with fine sandpaper, taking great care not to scrape the surface of the surrounding glaze. If the filling of the mould has been neatly done, there should not be much sanding to do.

Gravers can be used to sharpen the detail of a design. Examine for small holes in the surface, or round the edge of the filling, where it meets the porcelain. These must be filled with a softer version of the mixture used for the main filling. Smooth the composition evenly, making sure that the holes, if any, are properly filled. A little more sanding will be necessary when this has dried.

Filling in pottery   Pottery can be filled in with plaster of Paris mixed with water alone, plaster of Paris mixed with water to which has been added a little polyvinyl acetate emulsion, or with Polyfilla and Fine Surface Polyfilla. Powder pigments can be added to all of these.

To mix plaster of Paris, *add the plaster to the water*. Have the water in a small flexible container, sprinkle the plaster into the water, a little at a time, to avoid lumps. When a mound of plaster can be seen coming almost to the top of the water level, stop adding plaster. Stir gently to ascertain the texture of the mixture. Plaster must not be added after the stirring has begun, so if the mixture is still runny, leave for a little while to allow the plaster to absorb more water. Keep an eye on it and when it is a soft, creamy texture it is ready to use. If a tinted filling is needed, the powder colours should be added to the dry plaster. It is difficult to judge exactly the amount of colour to add because the filling will dry considerably lighter. Test the colour by adding some of the tinted plaster to a minute amount of water. Place this mixture on a piece of white paper and dry near heat. Add more colour or plaster as needed. Experimenting is the only way to overcome the problem. If a filling dries too light, pare it down below the level of the ceramic and apply a second, slightly darker layer of tinted filling.

Plasticine (Roma Plastelina) can be used as a simple support for the plaster fillings, as well as for the Polyfilla ones. Before fitting the Plasticine (Roma Plastelina) to the object, wet the edges of the pottery thoroughly, then apply some P.V.A. adhesive to assist the bond of the filling. Dry the pottery on either side of the gap so that the Plasticine (Roma Pastelina) will adhere. Fit the Plasticine (Roma Plastelina) into place, dust with talc then fill with whichever filling is being used, plaster of Paris, plaster and P.V.A., or Polyfilla. Smooth the surface with a spatula dipped in water and leave to dry. Sand as much as necessary to bring the plaster surface level with the ceramic.

For very coarse pottery or stoneware a little marble flour (marble powder) or some fine, clean sand may be added to improve the texture, Plaster, mixed with water and a little P.V.A., is used in the same way as plaster. This filling can be built up in layers, but it dries quickly, so mix in fairly small quantities and use at once. Add the powder colours as before.

Polyfilla is self-adhesive so it too can be built up in layers. It will also adhere to the pottery but a little P.V.A. can be applied to the edges of the pottery if it is thought that extra adhesive would be advisable, for example if the missing part is extensive. Polyfilla can be sanded but the surface will not be as good as plaster. This can be an advantage if the pottery is very coarse, but if a finer textured surface is required Fine Surface Polyfilla can be added as a final layer over the Polyfilla. A little sanding will give an excellent surface. As with plaster the addition of the powder pigments is difficult because both Polyfillas dry lighter. Again the restorer will have to experiment, using the test suggested for plaster.

Moulds to assist filling in missed pieces Having dealt with cracks, chips and other small missing areas it is time to consider extensive restorations which need more complicated moulds. Impressions must be taken of handles, limbs, openwork borders, flowers, and many other sections which the restorer will eventually be called upon to repair. Some of these moulds will be made, then filled, and the resulting reproduction bonded onto the object. Other moulds will be attached to the broken objects and filled in place.

The dental impression compound, Paribar (Mercaptan), although not suitable for extensive repairs, has more uses as a moulding material than Plasticine (Roma Plastelina). It is hard and inflexible when cold so cannot be used for lattice work or very curved sections, or complicated things like flowers and hands, where a flexible moulding material would be much better. (Mercaptan is more flexible than Paribar.)

Paribar comes in round cakes which look like toffee. (Mercaptan is a two-part material. Follow mixing instructions, working quickly, then use as described for Paribar.) To prepare it for use, put a cake in a bowl of very hot (not boiling) water until soft enough to mould with the hands. When the material is even-textured and has been worked into the required shape, allowing enough to overlap the missing section, it will probably have become semi-hard so put it back into hot water for a few minutes until thoroughly soft. Quickly press into place over the pattern section and allow to set until firm enough to hold the impression, but not totally hard. Remove with care, easing it up and out from the ceramic, and allow to finish hardening. Paribar (Mercaptan) does not need a separator (see Glossary) either from the ceramic or from the filling. The area from which the impression is taken must be identical with the missing area. If the object has a raised design make sure that the mould covers and overlaps by about 1·25 cm ($\frac{1}{2}$ in) that part of the design which corresponds with the missing section. When applying the moulding compound to the pattern, assuming that the damaged area is on the edge of the piece, make sure that the impression includes the rim of the object so that the mould will have the correct outline. This will also ensure accurate placing of the mould on the damaged area and save work when the time comes to sand the dry filling. At the same time, do not bring the edge of the mould so far over the rim that, when it is being removed from the object, it becomes locked into place. This could happen also if the raised pattern on the object is in high relief.

If the mould has been correctly made it should fit snugly against the ceramic and over the gap, and feel as though it belongs there. If the fit is not good it must be re-made, by softening the impression compound and starting again. Once the mould is in place it is filled in the same way as the small chips when Plasticine (Roma Plastelina) or tape were used as a support: by applying some thin composition to the broken edges, then filling the mould with the firm composition. The mould can be filled away from the object, allowed to dry and the new piece then bonded into place. This makes an extra stage and is not really necessary with this type of mould. More complicated moulds, using different materials, on objects like hands and arms, *are* made and applied separately because they are complete in themselves, and are not sections missing out of a given area. When the filling is dry remove the mould. As before there will be a certain amount of sanding and sharpening of detail to be done. Use gravers, needle files and sandpaper to improve the surface and to make certain that the join is even. *Don't* sand below the level of the ceramic, *don't* scratch the glaze. *Do* work away from the ceramic with both the tools and the sandpaper, *do* keep looking to see how much work is left to be done, *don't* stay in one little area of the repair so that the level becomes uneven. When sanding the underneath of a foot rim, stand the object on the sandpaper and turn it between the hands to achieve an even surface. Almost certainly there will be air holes and small patches round the edge of the join which will have to be filled again with a soft mixture. When all the sanding, filing and filling has been accomplished, polish the whole area with Solvol Autosol to provide a good surface for the glaze medium. If great care is exercised, abrasive drills fitted into a flexible shaft drill can be used to grind down composition, but only where they can reach without damaging the surrounding ceramic. They must in any case, be used very judiciously. If, as sometimes happens, too much composition has been applied, the drill can be used to grind it down without wasting time laboriously sanding it.

Rubber latex moulds These moulds are used to take casts for missing flowers, handles, hands, arms, feet, and even heads, although this is rare. Heads can be successfully replaced, but it is unlikely that the restorer will have to do it often, either for himself or for customers. Very few people would care to be the owners of a figure with a completely new head, whereas a few new fingers or even a new arm or foot are acceptable.

There are two moulding materials used in this area of restoration, rubber latex moulds (Qualitex PV rubber latex or Revultex rubber latex (Pliatex), described in materials list, page 32) and silicone rubber moulds to be discussed a little later Rhodorsil RTV 11 504 A or Silastomer 9161 (Silastic 3110), see materials list, page 33). The former are flexible, and very versatile, in that they can be used for many different shapes of mould. For very small moulds, such as flowers, they are used without the addition of a thickener and do not need a support. Using a small, fairly stiff brush, the first layer of creamy white mixture is coaxed smoothly onto the pattern in a thin layer, avoiding air bubbles, and left to dry for several hours, depending on the thickness of the layer and the temperature of the room. As the rubber dries it turns brown. A second layer is painted over the first and again left to dry. Four to six layers should provide a strong enough mould for a small area like that of a flower. However, if it is desired to speed up the making of the mould, or to make it stronger, minute snippets of cotton wool, butter-muslin or cheese-cloth, can be mixed into the latex before it is applied to the ceramic. If this thickened mixture is to be used, it must be painted over a first layer of unthickened latex, which will provide a smooth surface to the inside of the mould. One, or at the most two, layers of the thickened mixture are applied as soon as the first layer is dry. When the latex is used for taking a cast of an extensive area on, say, a large dish cover or a large bowl, it will be necessary to provide a support, or 'mother', for the mould. Make a latex mould which is fairly thick but still flexible enough to be removed *safely* from the pattern piece. The back of the mould is then coated with a layer of plaster of Paris (mixed as described earlier in this chapter, on page 62), approximately 0·625 cm ($\frac{1}{4}$ in) deep. Set aside until the plaster is absolutely dry. If the plaster is removed from the latex before it is hard it will break and a new support will have to be made. Sometimes, especially with a large mould, it may be difficult to release the plaster from the latex, so coat the *back* of the mould with a little Slipwax release agent (Butcher's Wax) (see page 35) before applying the plaster. When ready to use the mould, dust the inside with talc and fit it back into its 'mother'. Then fit both the latex mould and its support to the area to be repaired, strapping them onto the object with Scotch tape if necessary, to keep them firmly in position. As before, apply a minute amount of thin composition to the broken edges and then line the mould with thin composition, followed by a firm mixture.

Making a mould of an arm is a rather tricky procedure which requires skill and patience. The mould must be in one piece, i.e. it will look like a small tube when finished. It must be strong enough to retain the shape of the arm, but must also be flexible enough to be removed from the arm without damaging the fingers. Do not thicken the latex because bulk must be avoided. Depending upon the thickness of each application it will take from five to six layers. The latex is very inclined to stick to itself so liberal dustings of talc must be applied once the last layer has dried, so that the mould can be rolled back onto itself and gradually worked down the arm, and over the fingers. Working the mould off the fingers is the difficult part, because tiny porcelain fingers are so easily broken. Nevertheless, it can be successfully accomplished if sufficient care is exercised and the whole operation is done very slowly.

Direct modelling Where a pattern is not obtainable for an arm, or a hand only, the restorer's skill and ingenuity will be called into action and he will have to model the missing limb from a photograph, or even from his own drawing. Photographs can often be found in books if the figure is an interesting piece, or they can sometimes be obtained from a museum. Occasionally drawings can be made from a piece seen in a collection. In exceptional cases the restorer may be allowed to make a mould on a museum piece.

Direct modelling can be done in two ways. It can be built up over a metal pin, using several layers of Araldite or Ablebond 342-1 composition until the desired result is achieved (a method which will be discussed later in this section), or a limb can be modelled in Plasticine (Roma Plastelina) or modelling wax on which a mould can be made in the same way as it was when a pattern was available. Starting with a piece of Plasticine (Roma Plastelina), or wax, rather larger than the size of the finished arm, roll it into a cylindrical shape. The modelling will have to be done by holding the cylinder in one hand and modelling with the other, using the boxwood modelling tool, and small pointed instruments such as dental hand tools for fingers and fine detail. It is here that a knowledge of sculpture and how to shape a piece of clay-like material into a form resembling an arm or hand, is necessary. Begin by looking at the style of modelling of the remaining arm (assuming that there is one!) on the figure to be restored. Notice whether the bone structure is pronounced, or just suggested in the simplest possible way. No matter how simple the modelling may *appear*, further investigation will show that the original modeller knew his anatomy. In talking about modelling a new limb, it is taken for granted that the figure to be restored is of sufficient quality to warrant the amount of work involved, and would therefore be of a high standard of modelling. If both arms are missing, try to find a figure from the same factory and by the same modeller, if known, in a museum and take note of the style of modelling. If the second arm is present, take measurements with callipers and dividers, marking them down on a piece of paper and noting which measurement is which, e.g. shoulder to elbow, elbow to wrist, etc., and the diameters of elbows, wrists, fingers, and any other measurements which could be helpful in achieving an accurate reproduction of the limb. As the modelling proceeds, keep checking the measurements on the modelling material with the callipers and the dividers.

Using the rubber latex emulsion moulding material, make a mould on the modelled arm in the same way as was explained for the porcelain pattern (page 67). Don't forget to apply talc to the rubber before removing it from the arm. Dust the inside of the mould with talc making sure that none collects at the bottom of the fingers. Filling a tube-shaped mould is somewhat different from filling an open mould. The composition must be thin so that it will flow down into the fingers, which are very small. Araldite AY 103 with hardener HY 956 or Ablebond 342-1 parts A and B are good for this, but Two-Tube Araldite (Devcon '2-ton') can be used if the mixture is kept thin, and warming the composition just before pouring will help. When the composition has been mixed drip a small amount from the tip of the metal spatula into the mould, trying to run it down the side so that it will not cause an air block as it travels to the fingers. Getting the mixture to settle evenly in the fingers without creating air bubbles can be a problem. This can be overcome by squeezing the tips of the fingers after each addition of composition; the air will thus be expelled and the fingers gradually filled. Once the filling reaches the wrist the worst is over, but it is still advisable to add the mixture gradually. Flicking the mould with the fingers or tapping it lightly on the table will keep the air bubbles on the move. Push a

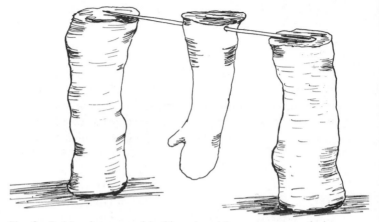

Fig. 8. Rubber latex mould of hand and forearm suspended between two pads of Plasticine (Roma Plastelina)

needle through the edges of the mould at the top and suspend between two blocks of Plasticine (Roma Plastelina) so that the composition can dry without being disturbed.

When the time comes to peel off the rubber mould—after twenty-four hours, or as much as three days for Araldite AY 103 or Ablebond 342-1—the utmost care must always be taken when the fingers are reached. They are at least as fragile as they are in porcelain. It may be necessary to slit the rubber with a sharp blade, but be careful not to cut the fingers inside at the same time!

Silicone rubber moulds Silicone rubber moulds are not as flexible as the latex rubber moulds, therefore they are not as versatile, and they are more difficult to use in that a catalyst has to be mixed with the silicone. It is important to make sure that there are no undercuts on the area of ceramic from which a mould is to be taken—in other words, nothing that would obstruct the removal of the mould. If the rubber is locked into place by a piece of ceramic, either the mould would have to be cut off, and so spoilt, or the ceramic would be broken. This can be overcome by packing the gap underneath the obstructing

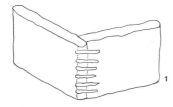 

Fig. 9. Preparing a Plasticine (Roma Plastelina) box to hold a silicone rubber mould.
1. Where the edges of two flat pieces of Plasticine butt they are gashed with a boxwood modelling tool
2. The surface is then smoothed over to make a leak-proof join

piece of ceramic with Plasticine (Roma Plastelina), thus preventing the rubber from becoming trapped.

Best results are obtained with silicone rubber moulds if they are poured into a 'box' made from Plasticine (Roma Plastelina). Walls of this material are built round the area from which the mould is to be taken, extending beyond that area by about 1·25 cm ($\frac{1}{2}$ in) depending on the size of the mould required. Obviously a small flower would not need a mould with a 1·25 cm ($\frac{1}{2}$ in) border so the restorer's own judgment must be used. All joins in the Plasticine (Roma Plastelina) must be sealed by making small slashes across the seams and then smoothing them flat, using a boxwood modelling tool. Where the Plasticine (Roma Plastelina) meets the ceramic, smear it down onto the glaze to seal the joins and prevent any rubber escaping. The two brands of silicone rubber mould are equally good but both must be mixed with care, using 5 per cent catalyst to rubber (ten parts Silastic 3110 to one part Catalyst 1 by weight). There is a tendency with these moulds to form air bubbles during the mixing process. By using a flat blade and working the mixture very slowly, this can be reduced. When pouring the rubber into the Plasticine (Roma Plastelina) 'box', run it down the sides and tap the object with a finger, or stop every so often and move it backwards and forwards, taking care not to damage either the object or the mould. By disturbing the mixture in the 'box' the air bubbles are forced to the top. Air bubbles in the mould would cause holes in the cast, which would have to be filled in with further composition. One or two bubbles will probably remain trapped in the rubber, no matter how much care is taken.

The depth of the rubber is determined by the area of the mould. If the mould is small, about 0·625 cm ($\frac{1}{4}$ in) will suffice, but if the mould is large it must be at least 188 cm ($\frac{3}{4}$ in) thick. Try not to make it so thick that it will be absolutely rigid, but there must be sufficient thickness for the rubber to hold the shape of the object from which the impression is being taken. Only practice will ensure that the restorer makes his moulds of exactly the right strength. The rubber should be allowed to dry for about twenty-four hours before removal from the pattern. It must then be further cured in the oven at a temperature of 65°C (150°F) for one hour. Air-drying does not completely dry the rubber, so the period in the oven will prevent the composition filling from sticking to the mould. As with the latex rubber moulds, the silicone rubber moulds are dusted with talc before filling with the composition. They can be filled after the mould has been strapped into place on the object or filled separately and the piece of composition bonded onto the ceramic later.

Two-piece moulds Silicone rubber moulds can be made in two sections and this is a useful method when reproducing handles. A Plasticine (Roma Plastelina) 'box' which is built round the handle, lengthwise, leaving half of the handle exposed, serves as a container for the silicone rubber. Shallow holes are made in the Plasticine (Roma Plastelina) which will form keys in the rubber. When the rubber has set, the Plasticine (Roma Plastelina) is removed, and a wall is built round the first half of the mould, which also serves as the floor of the second half of the mould. The surface of the rubber *edges* must be dusted with talc or smeared lightly with Silicone release agent (Butcher's Wax) to prevent the two halves sticking together. A second mixing of rubber is poured into the box and left to set. The two halves are then separated and put into the oven to cure, before filling with composition as before. This process is

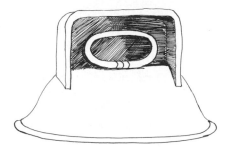

Fig. 10. Plasticine (Roma Plastelina) box prepared to receive silicone rubber moulding material

described in detail in the section called 'Restoring a Derby Vase', page 111.

Reinforcing and dowelling Reinforcing means the insertion of brass or stainless steel rods into the ceramic either to support composition when modelling directly onto an object, or as dowels when a very heavy piece is being reassembled. Holes are drilled into the ceramic in both cases, a soft mixture of composition is put into the holes and the dowels or pins fitted into place. Diamond pointed instruments are fitted into the flexible shaft drill. Use a small point just to *start* the holes, then fit larger instruments to drill to the required diameter and depth.

The most important aspects of making dowels and pins are the size, depth, and position of the drilled holes, and then the size of the dowels, or pins, in relation to the holes. The thickness of the ceramic at the broken edges determines the dimensions of the holes to be drilled, and the soft stainless steel or half hard brass wire rods are cut to fit the holes. The area surrounding the dowel hole must, on all sides, have a width not less than the diameter of the hole. A rough guide for the length of the dowel is that both sections, i.e., the part embedded in the ceramic and the part embedded in the new section or the other piece of ceramic, should be not less than three times the diameter of the dowel. The gauges of wire that will be the most useful are 11G to 18G or 19G, the lower figure being the heavier gauge.

It is recommended that the restorer practise drilling on an old plate of no value, before attempting to drill holes for dowels on a valuable object. Control of the drill must be developed so that when drilling on objects of value it is not allowed to slip on the glaze and cause irreparable damage. Cheap plates can be bought at Woolworths. While practice is advisable, the restorer will at the same time not wish to wear out expensive diamond drills. The drills must also be protected from overheating by the use of water. A mechanically minded restorer could easily suspend an upturned plastic bottle, fitted with a piece of fine tubing, so that water drips onto the spot where the drill is working; or perhaps a friend could be persuaded to help with this important detail.

Starting with a heavy plate, or dish, as the first exercise in dowelling, measure the *thickness* of the ceramic, divide it by three, and that will be the diameter of the hole. Multiply the diameter by three and that will be the depth of the holes to be drilled. The positioning of the holes must now be decided. Avoid areas where the ceramic is thin and do not drill near the rim of the plate. On a very large dish four or five dowels may be needed, but on a plate of 11–12 in (27·5–30 cm), three or four will be sufficient. Since the joins will also be bonded, the dowels will act as join *strengtheners* and will not be bearing all the strain. Mark the positions of the holes, using a brightly coloured paint (not oils), or a volatile crayon (china marking pencil). Next, bring the second half of the object in contact with the first, thereby marking off the hole positions onto the other half, and ensuring accuracy. Starting with a small-pointed drill, begin each hole, working very gently when the drill first comes in contact with the ceramic. Once the holes have been started and a larger drill has been fitted, the drilling should be comparatively easy. Don't forget to use water while drilling, *at all times*. Drill all the holes on both edges. At this stage the dowels must be cut to size and fitted into the holes with the pieces in position. When the dowels are the correct length, file

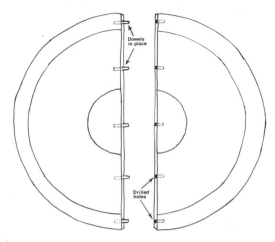

Fig. 11. Dowelling a plate

each end flat, and roughen the surfaces with a coarse file. This will give the composition extra purchase on the dowels.

Mix the composition, thinly for bonding the edges of the join, and a little thicker for setting the dowels in their holes. If the object is for everyday use, it would be advisable to use Two-Tube Araldite (Devcon '2-ton'). If, however, the object is of value, use Araldite AY 103 or Ablebond 342-1 with Hardener HY 956. If using Two-Tube Araldite (Devcon '2-ton'), keep the mixture thin, using only a little titanium dioxide, plus some pigment to bring the mixture as near as possible to the colour of the ceramic. If the mixture is too thick it will obstruct the close fitting of the pieces. When fitting the dowels into their holes make sure that the thicker composition does not exude above the level of the holes. If using Araldite AY 103 or Ablebond 342-1 always allow it to stand for an hour or a little longer, depending on the temperature of the room. It should be starting to thicken, and it helps to stir the adhesive mixture occasionally. Spread one edge with the thin composition, then put some thicker mixture into the dowel holes and press the dowels into position. Place this half in the sand box so that both hands are free to handle the second half. Fill the remaining holes with composition and very gently bring the second half into contact with the first. To hold the two halves in the correct position it is necessary to tape them back and front. Leave the object in the sand box for about six hours for the Two-Tube Araldite (Devcon '2-ton') mixture, but for a minimum of twenty-four hours in the case of Araldite AY 103 or Ablebond 342-1. It could even take as long as three days for the AY 103 to harden in the dowel holes. There are many different occasions when dowels will be needed to strengthen joins—legs to bodies, arm sections to the rest of an arm, heads to necks, handles to cups and jugs, to mention a few examples. The restorer will learn to judge when a dowel is necessary, but the following suggestions can be used as a guide. Where a join falls in an awkward place such as an elbow or a knee; in any situation where a bonded join would be carrying too much strain without the aid of dowels; to fit a composition handle to a cup or jug, with half the dowel in the ceramic and half in the new handle. In each case, the process is the same for the heavy plate or dish—one edge of the join is covered with tinted composition, the dowel holes are filled with composition on each side, the dowels are pressed into position and the edges are then brought together and strapped securely in place.

Pinning The procedure with pinning is slightly different. A pin is used as a support for direct modelling. There is only one edge of ceramic because the other is missing completely. The length of the pin is decided by the length of the missing section. If the part to be modelled is an arm, the length is measured, taking into account the curve of the elbow, and the length of the hand as far as the *knuckles*, plus the amount of wire that is to be embedded in the ceramic. The latter is decided on the same principle as for a dowel, not less than three times the diameter of the pin must be allowed, plus a little extra if the depth of the ceramic will permit. Great care must be taken when drilling into a shoulder because the diamond instrument could suddenly reach a hollow area, and the shock of suddenly breaking through could damage it. Usually it is possible to tell

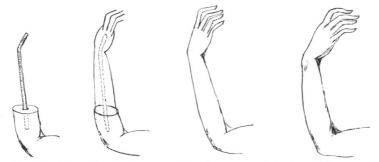

Fig. 12. Modelling forearm and hand over a metal pin and fine wire finger supports

when the drill is reaching a hollow place because it feels as though the drill is about to break through the ceramic, a sensation akin to that of walking on thin ice! Avoid, if possible, drilling through into the hollow area by stopping the drill as soon as a change in 'sensation' is felt. If the ceramic does break through into the shoulder area, the pin is bonded into place, with a section protruding into the hollow area if necessary to provide the correct amount of length, and using extra composition to fill the gap. Once the pin is bonded into place and the composition is dry, the modelling can begin. Make a firm mixture of composition (reserving a little thin mixture to smear onto the wire), using Araldite AY 103 or Ablebond 342-1 with titanium dioxide powder, and either some kaolin or barytes powder. Do not make the mixture so firm that it will not adhere to the pin, but it must be possible to roll it out on the sheet of plate glass without sticking, using a little kaolin or barytes as 'flour'. Apply a little composition to the *roughened* surface of the pin over the adhesive. Roll out a narrow strip of the composition and wind it onto the pin, to reach as far as the knuckles. It must now be left to harden before a second layer can be added. It will not be possible to do much shaping with the first layer, but bear in mind that less material will be needed at slim places such as the wrist. Again mix a firm composition and begin modelling the arm, using the measurements taken from the other arm or from a pattern piece, or use the eye to

judge the proportions from a photograph. Remember that the
pin reaches only as far as the knuckles so that extra pins must be
added, one for each of the fingers. If the figure is large, very fine
dowelling wire can be used, gauge 18G or 19G, but on the
whole electrical wire will be the most useful for this purpose.
Choose from the three gauges, 30G, 33G, or 38G (see page 23),
according to the size of the fingers to be modelled. When the
modelling of the arm and hand has been completed as far as the
knuckles, careful measurements having been taken throughout,
the pins for the fingers can be fitted into the still soft
composition. The wire should reach *just short of the tips of the
fingers* so that there will be room for a small pad of composition
to cover the end of the wire. When the final layer of composition
has hardened, the surface and the finer points of the modelling
can be done with sandpaper, gravers and files. A useful
implement is made by wrapping sandpaper round a modelling
tool. The sandpaper can also be folded into any shape to fit the
needs of the moment. Check the join for accuracy and refill if
necessary. When the new arm has reached the required
standard, the surface can be polished with Solvol Autosol, after
which it will be ready for the first layer of paint.

10. Colour-matching, painting and glazing

Colour-matching and the application of the paint will test the beginner's skills to the utmost. Both procedures may, at first consideration, seem simple, but there is a great deal more work involved than most people realize. It is this area of restoration which takes up so much time and for which restorers have to charge so highly. The layman finds it hard to envisage the time, skill and patience which are required to accomplish this part of the restoration process successfully. The ground colour, for instance, is not applied in one layer; it is gradually built up in two, three and sometimes as many as five or six layers. The first layer requires a high percentage of white pigment, which is the only one which will disguise the repair. Some colours are extremely difficult to duplicate. Again, the actual application of the paint is far more complicated than is generally supposed. It takes time and much practice to master the hand painting techniques which are so different from other forms of painting, and the airbrush demands patience, and even more practice. The answer is to start with small areas, preferably on pottery, which will give good results more quickly than porcelain, although soft-paste porcelain is comparatively easy. Why not start on a Staffordshire group? Or a pastille burner in the shape of a castle? Or a modern pottery ashtray? Or a plate with a surface chip in a coloured area? These are just suggestions, and it really depends on what is available. Before starting to paint a repair, experiment with colours and brush strokes on plain white tiles. These are cheap and it would be worth while buying half a dozen. After mixing a colour successfully, dab some of it onto a tile. Beside it put a piece of brown adhesive packing tape and write down the combination of paints used, and the type of porcelain matched. These will be useful for reference, but in time colour-matching will become instinctive.

It is important to bear in mind the purposes served by overpainting and glazing, namely, to disguise and protect the repair. The first layer, with the high percentage of white pigment should, if possible, cover the repair so that the outlines cannot be seen. Sometimes it is necessary to incorporate some white into the second layer, and even the third. If this can be avoided, so much the better, because the layers of paint should be kept to the minimum. The first layer can contain a small amount of coloured pigment, although not, of course, for a white background. Seldom, though, is a 'white' ground entirely white—it almost always contains a tinge of colour, which can be simulated by applying a final clear glaze with a minute quantity of coloured pigment. So a coloured ceramic surface is simulated, whether it be pottery or porcelain, by gradually eliminating the white as the layers of paint are applied, at the same time increasing the amounts of coloured pigment.

Painting materials Assemble the tubes of oil colour, the jars of powder pigments, and the glaze mediums—Chintex for any wares which are going to be used, Chinaglaze Clear Gloss, for all other porcelain and for pottery as well, and Bedacryl 122X (Acryloid B48N) for pottery only. The Chintex clear glaze will of course need its thinner and the Chintex brush cleaner; the Chinaglaze Clear Gloss will need Phenthin 83, and Bedacryl 122X (Acryloid B48N) will need Xylene for its thinner, together with Cellosolve solvent to improve the flow. Keep all the powder pigments together, perhaps on a small tray; to keep the oil colours from being squashed, keep them in their boxes, in colour sequence—blues together and so on. Oil colours can be used successfully with the glaze mediums, especially the Chintex clear glaze. However, it is a good idea to get rid of as much of the oil as possible. (See page 34.) To this list add a palette knife, a piece of plate glass or a porcelain paint dish, sable brushes, silk and cotton rags, magnifying glass, a fine needle or very fine pointed tweezers, and an old, stiff brush for mixing. To practise colour-matching, gather together some pieces of pottery and porcelain and try to work out which paints to combine for each area of colour, remembering to keep samples on the tiles as suggested. It will not be easy at first, but the only way to learn is to mix and match, mix and match.

The list of colours in the chapter dealing with materials (see page 33) is adequate for the restorer's needs, although he will, no doubt, find others that he will add to the list. To apply colour to pottery and porcelain, a glaze medium is needed with which to mix the colours, whether oil, or powder pigments. Oil paints on their own would only rub off in a short space of time and powder colours would be quite useless without a medium.

To bake or not to bake At this stage a decision has to be made as to which glaze medium is to be used. The restorer must ask himself whether the piece is for purely ornamental use, or whether it is to be used in the kitchen where it will have to withstand washing in detergents, and hot water. If the latter, then baking with a glaze medium that will take a considerable amount of wear and tear is advised, but it must be remembered that no restoration, however good, will be as strong as the original ceramic. It is, after all, only a reconstruction. As far as decorative wares are concerned, hard-paste porcelain can be baked, using Chintex clear glaze, if desired. It is recommended that all antique pottery and porcelain be retouched, or even overpainted, with the Chinaglaze Clear Gloss air-drying lacquer, or Bedacryl 122X (Acryloid B48N). It is unnecessary to bake decorative wares and, in the case of soft-paste porcelain, baking can cause irreparable damage, such as discoloration, and minute cracks appear as if by magic. Chinaglaze Clear Gloss works very well for both pottery and porcelain, and Bedacryl 122X (Acryloid B48N) is useful on the type of pottery which has a very thick glaze. Bedacryl (Acryloid B48N) *can* be used for porcelain but requires great skill in application.

With all overpainting it must be borne in mind that the area of paint must be kept to the minimum conducive to the achievement of a good surface, and at the same time obliterate the repair beneath. The first layer of paint must extend *fractionally* beyond the repair, and then be faded, or feathered, out so that it does not form a ridge. When the paint layer has dried, either by baking in the oven in the case of Chintex, or air-drying in the case of Chinaglaze Clear Gloss and Bedacryl 122X (Acryloid B48N), it is gently sanded with a fine sandpaper or Flexigrit A400, to remove particles of pigment which did not blend in sufficiently with the glaze medium, and to smooth down ridges, if any. Each layer is treated in this way until the final one, which should be blemish free and have blended well with the surrounding glaze.

The first exercise in painting Let us use a Staffordshire group as a first exercise in painting. Either Chinaglaze Clear Gloss or alternatively Bedacryl 122X (Acryloid B48N) would be suitable, but the Chinaglaze Clear Gloss is very much easier to use and covers all the needs of a piece of this type. Mix Chinaglaze Clear Gloss with some titanium dioxide powder on the plate glass palette, using an old, stiff bristle paint brush or a palette knife. A white tile can also be used, as can a porcelain paint dish, but the latter is only suitable for very small quantities. Make sure that the medium and the white pigment are *very thoroughly*

Fig. 13. Powder pigments must be very thoroughly mixed with the glaze medium

mixed so that no lumps appear in the paint surface. It will probably be necessary to add a little thinner to the mixture, but do not make it too thin. Remember that the first mixture must be sufficiently opaque to obliterate the repair. Another point which should be self-evident: *do not* put wet brushes into the jars of pigments, or paint-covered brushes into the glaze mediums or solvents. For easier handling, small quantities of the mediums should be decanted into small jars, and a *clean* palette knife can then be dipped in for the required amount. The metal spatula makes a good dispenser for the powder pigments. These may seem to be fussy details, but cleanliness and neatness play a very important part in the painting process.

Once the glaze medium and the white pigment have been thoroughly mixed it is time to decide which coloured pigments to use. Staffordshire figures do have very light background colours, but they are never completely white. Look at the ground colour very carefully, with a magnifying glass if necessary. A faint tint of blue or green will probably be seen in the original glaze and this is applied in the final layer of painted glaze. A small amount of colour will be required in the white layer—perhaps a touch of yellow ochre and burnt umber, and a *suspicion* of light red. The colour is provided by the pottery showing through the glaze. The rich, dark blue found on so many Staffordshire figures is achieved by mixing a certain amount of ultramarine blue with the first mainly white layer. It should be possible to dispense with the white by a third layer, gradually deepening the blue and adding a *minute* amount of alizarin crimson, and even a speck of black, until the required depth of colour is reached. A final layer, or perhaps two, of clear glaze will give the thickly glazed look. The bright orange also found on these figures and groups can be achieved by mixing aureolin yellow with small amounts of cadmium red and burnt sienna, and occasionally burnt umber to darken it. Always smudge a little of the paint mixture onto the glaze, well away from the repaired area, to see if it is a good match. Before applying the paint to the repair, stop and think! The paint must be applied without leaving brush strokes, or pools of colour which will take a long time to dry out, and make the sanding process much longer than necessary. Decide on the direction in which the brush is to travel, towards the restorer or away from him, and the exact spot where the paint is to be faded out. The application of paint can be described as 'coaxing' rather than painting, and it will help to think of this while working. Have a fine brush ready with which to feather the edges. Apply the layer as smoothly as possible, and, working quickly, draw the edge of the paint softly onto the surface of the glaze with the small brush which has been dipped in a *thinned* mixture of clear glaze. Be careful not to bring the edges further than necessary onto the original glaze because other layers must follow and the end result will be an area of painted glaze which reaches too far beyond the area of the repair. Smudging the edges with a silk rag will sometimes work, and even the tip of the small finger can be used to thin out the paint. This is something which can be practised on a tile. The secret of feathering, or fading, the edges of the paint is lightness of touch, and speed. The less pigment there is in the glaze medium the easier will be the feathering operation, thus the final layer of clear glaze will, or should, be invisibly faded out.

Hints for successful painting A good order of working is to paint each area of repair with opaque white base colour, tinted where necessary, and then set the piece aside to dry. Next, add a further layer to each section, and so on until all the repaired areas are ready for their final glaze. If the work is carried out in this systematic way from the beginning, it will become a habit which will serve the restorer well when he finds himself working on many different objects. It will save time and help to prevent one area falling behind, and having to mix a special batch of paint.

Hand painting proceeds as described above, no matter which type of ceramic, with slight variations according to the glaze medium. Just remember to keep the paint within bounds and take great care to mix the colours as accurately as possible. Light plays an important part in colour-mixing. Most blues change in different lighting and the safest way to achieve the right colour is to work in a north light. Fluorescent light works well with many colours but is unreliable with blues and the type of yellow-browns found on T'ang pottery and the Imperial Yellow Chinese porcelain. If at all possible, work in the same type of lighting as will be found where the object is to be displayed. A change of ownership and, inevitably, lighting, may show up a hitherto unnoticeable repair. A word of warning: resist the temptation to rush ahead. To complete successfully one stage of painting on each job in hand is enough for each day. The paint *must* be allowed to *dry thoroughly* before the application of the next layer.

Painting with Chintex Chintex clear glaze requires careful application, using the same basic technique as was described earlier. This glaze does have a tendency to form air bubbles: a point which must be watched. Particular care in the preparation of the surface will help to guard against the formation of air bubbles, and the application of a first coat of clear glaze, without any pigment whatsoever, will provide a smooth surface for the first layer of pigmented glaze. Make sure that pools of glaze do not collect in dips or pockets in the ceramic—these would automatically form bubbles. Sand between each application. Chintex clear glaze has, of course, to be baked in the domestic oven at 94°C (220°F) for half an hour after each coat of glaze has been applied, except the last one when the object is left in the oven for an hour. Towards the end of each baking time turn off the oven and allow it to cool, leaving the object in the oven for about twenty minutes beyond the actual baking time. The reason for this is that the shock of being removed from the heat of the oven to a much lower temperature could cause some types of porcelain to crack. If, when the object is removed from the oven, it is seen that air bubbles have burst, leaving small holes in the surface of the glaze, they must be dealt with before a further coat of paint is applied. While the piece is still warm (*not* hot), dip a fine paint brush in clear glaze medium and drip small quantities into the holes in the glaze. The glaze will be sucked into the holes, and, after a further coat of paint over the entire repaired area, and another baking, they should have disappeared. If they persist, as sometimes happens, repeat the process until they have been eliminated. A separate baking after filling the holes with glaze is permissible, but should be avoided if possible because the number of baking periods should be kept to the minimum.

Painting with Bedacryl 122X (Acryloid B48N) Bedacryl 122X (Acryloid B48N) is a difficult medium to use, but it does have its advantages. It is water white, does not discolour with age, and is particularly good for pottery, especially where the glaze is thick and shiny. It is not advisable to use Bedacryl 122X (Acryloid B48N) with the airbrush, although not impossible if a small amount of Cellosolve solvent is mixed with it to improve the flow and lessen the 'orange-peeling'. Xylene is, of course, the thinner. Cellosolve solvent will also help to achieve a good surface when hand brushing Bedacryl 122X (Acryloid B48N). Do not attempt painting large areas of light ground colour with Bedacryl, certainly not to begin with, because considerable skill with the paint brush is required to manage this medium. Do not lay the Bedacryl 122X (Acryloid B48N) too thickly because it will take a very long time to dry, thus delaying the application of the next coat. For each layer the paint mixture should be thinned to a workable consistency, which could be described as a thin syrup, with Xylene and Cellosolve solvent. After each application the piece must be left to dry for several days, say a minimum of two, depending on the humidity of the weather. Drying time can be speeded up by placing the painted object in front of a sun lamp of the type that is used in the home. Do not put the piece nearer to the lamp than 45 cm (18 in). From time to time test the temperature of the object with the hand to make sure that it is not too hot.

Spray-painting or airbrushing Some people find spray-painting easier than painting by hand and others are happier using a paint brush. The airbrush should be kept for large areas of ground colour which would constitute an arduous task if attempted by hand. The other use for the airbrush is for painting handles, and arms and legs, where it would be difficult to achieve a smooth surface if the work were done by hand; painting by hand would take a long time, working right round the handle, or arm, before the paint had dried too much to allow a smooth blending of the paint. Whichever glaze medium is used with the airbrush, it must be thinned down a great deal more than for painting by hand—the best description being the consistency of milk. Thinning can be done either in the colour cup of the airbrush, or in a paint dish and then transferred to the cup, the latter being the easier way. **Caution:** the pigments must be particularly well combined with the glaze medium *before* the thinner is added, because lumps could block the airbrush nozzle, and hold up the work while it is taken apart and cleaned. If the glaze medium is difficult to mix with the pigments, a very little thinner may be added to make it more workable.

The principle of applying the paint is the same as when it is painted on by hand—a first layer of glaze medium with a high proportion of white pigment, followed by several more layers with the white pigment lessening as the layers increase, and the coloured pigments increasing until the required depth of colour is reached, and finishing with one or two layers of clear glaze medium, although the final layers can be tinted if necessary.

When the mixture has been thinned to the consistency of milk so that it will pass easily through the nozzle of the airbrush, practise using the airbrush on an old plate or a tile. Use circular movements, or work backwards and forwards in even lines which overlap each other. Keep the brush moving to prevent excessive accumulations of paint in one spot. Once the feel of the airbrush has been acquired, and a reasonable surface has been achieved, start painting a simple repair. A cup or jug handle would be a good object because there are definite starting and stopping points. Even if a little paint does spray onto the object itself it can easily be removed with the appropriate thinner. The arm on a figure is also easily painted with the airbrush, but do not allow an accumulation of paint between the fingers.

For small areas the airbrush is held fairly close to the surface, but not so close that the paint does not spread evenly. For larger areas it is held further away and the lever is pulled back to allow a greater flow of paint to leave the nozzle. For close painting the paint flow is limited to prevent build-up.

A problem A great problem with painting by airbrush is the overspray. This is the area at the edge of the paint which is slightly matt. Only the correct combination of glaze medium and thinner, air pressure, and the regulation of the volume of paint allowed to pass through the nozzle, can keep this area of overspray to the minimum. It is also lessened by gentle sanding between each layer of paint. Some restorers allow the pressure gauge to go as high as 60 lb (8·29 mks) per square inch, which is all right for painting large areas when the airbrush can be held away from the object and used with long sweeping movements. 50 lb (6·91 mks) of pressure is more manageable, and the airbrush can be used successfully with the pressure as low as 25 lb (3·46 mks). As with so many of the steps in restoration, much practice is required before mastery of the technique of airbrushing is attained. Do not despair, just keep trying. Once the pressure and paint flow have been decided for a particular piece, do not alter them, because this could cause an uneven surface. Practise varying the pressure and the paint flow, and the distance the airbrush is held from the object, noting the effects.

A spatter cup can be bought as an extra piece of equipment for the airbrush, for use on surfaces such as those found on some Chinese porcelain—blue glaze speckled with pale blue, and white, in very indefinite patterns which are extremely difficult to imitate by hand. By altering the shades of blue in the spatter cup this surface can be quite successfully copied. Spattering can also be achieved with the ordinary colour cup, sometimes inadvertently! Uneven dispersal of the powder pigments causing a blockage in the nozzle, or blockage by a bristle from a paint brush, or other foreign bodies are prime causes of unwanted spattering. If the glaze mixture is too thick, this also will block the nozzle and cause uneven spray. In each instance the colour cup will have to be emptied and the nozzle freed of whatever is obstructing it.

The lower the pressure the 'looser' the spray. This can be used to advantage if a 'watery' look is wanted, but the airbrush must be held away from the surface. To obtain a fine spray increase the pressure, still holding the airbrush away from the surface.

Decoration The painting of surfaces with the three different recommended glaze mediums has now been described, using both the hand brushing method and the airbrush. Decoration must now be considered. When discussing the painting of the Staffordshire group the application of several colours was shown to be a straightforward process. However, 'decoration' is seldom as simple as the patches of colour which are naïvely painted on so many examples of the type of Staffordshire pottery described. Decoration also implies straight lines, repeated designs which are often extremely complicated, the painting of flowers, parts of trees, and occasionally figures. Then there is 'crackle'—fine lines in the glaze, which are found on some Chinese wares, notably Celadon. Decoration also means imitation of the styles and methods of the original decorators, whether it is the way in which the hair was painted on a figure or the shading on a flower or leaf. It would be impossible to cover every type of decoration in so small a book, but ways of dealing with some of them can be mentioned in order to start the new restorer on his way. As knowledge accumulates, so will the ability to meet new challenges. No two pieces are alike and the restorer's ingenuity will be constantly taxed. If the restorer has no experience with a paint brush it will of course be difficult for him to paint complicated, repeated designs. This can be partly overcome by drawing the pattern lightly onto the painted (but *dry*) surface with a soft pencil, marking the repeat spots before starting to draw. It can also be

Fig. 14. A simple repeated pattern can be lightly pencilled in, whether for painting or gilding

done by tracing off the design from another area of the same object, or from a duplicate piece, using tracing paper and either a volatile crayon (china marking pencil) or a soft drawing pencil, then gently rubbing the back of the tracing paper in order to impress the design onto a piece of thin white paper. The white paper is then reversed and the back rubbed to transfer the design to the painted surface. This must be done carefully so as not to damage the paint. The process is not always entirely successful but missing lines can be filled in. Once the design is in place, it can be painted with a fine brush dipped in strong, thin colour. This is necessary so that a build-up of paint does not occur over the patterned areas. With underglaze blue, that is, a pattern applied in blue *under* the glaze, start painting the design on, say, the second layer of the ground colour, *just* overlapping the original at each end, so that it will be baked, or air dried, at the same time as the ground colour. It will then be sanded with the ground colour which will soften the edges of the blue design and help to merge it with its background. If this is done several times, until the correct depth of colour, both for the background and the blue design, is reached, the final layer, or two, of glaze medium can be applied and the appearance should be a good copy of the original.

'Crazing' and 'crackle' (see Glossary, page 132) can be copied

with either a pencil or the tip of a very fine paint brush. A pencil
works well for the very fine lines found in the pale cream glazes
of some types of T'ang figures and horses. For Chinese Celadon
wares, where the crackle is often brown in the green glaze, it is
better to use a oo sable brush, dipped in a thin, strongly
pigmented paint mixture. This takes a long time and is difficult
to execute successfully.

Straight lines are achieved with a steady hand, and even
breathing! Beginners tend to hold their breath, making it very
hard to keep the brush steady. Sometimes it is possible to rest
the middle finger of the painting hand on the rim of the object,
letting it move along with the fingers which are holding the
paint brush, thus creating a natural mahlstick. Sometimes it is
possible to use the handle of a long paint brush as a mahlstick, if
the object is large and heavy enough to rest on the table without
being held by the left hand. As with the repeated design, the
lines will have to overlap a very short distance onto the original.
Practise lines *before* attempting to paint them on objects. Veins
on leaves, lips, eyes, eyebrows, and hair on figures, minute
fabric designs on the clothes of many figures, and countless
other miniature exercises in painting will have to be done with a
oo sable brush. Use a thin but strongly pigmented paint

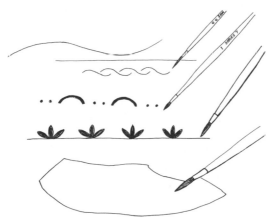

Fig. 15. Try to use the brush most suitable in size and shape

mixture and keep cleaning the brush to keep the fragile bristles
from becoming clogged, and so damaged. Eyebrows look more
realistic if they are painted from the outer tip inwards towards
the nose. Painted hair will also have a more natural look if the
brush is worked from the back of the head towards the front.
Lips and eyes should be kept slightly smaller than the original.
The less conspicuous they are the better. Flowers and leaves
come in so many varieties of colour and style that the restorer
will have to meet each challenge as it comes. Some leaves,
especially on porcelain groups, have been decorated in two
shades of green which run into each other. This can be imitated
by having the two shades of green already mixed, then painting
the lighter shade onto the restored leaf. While this first colour is
still wet, paint on the darker green, allowing it to merge at the
edges with the first colour. There is quite a knack to this little
exercise, but, once mastered, it will be very useful for flowers
too, where several shades of a colour, or sometimes one or two
different colours, merge into one another.

If a merging of colours occurs in extensive areas, the airbrush
can be used to good effect by spraying the colours into each
other while wet. Shading from dark to light, or vice versa, is also
successfully done with the airbrush, either by gradually
lightening or darkening the colour, or by holding the airbrush
nearer for the dark shades and further away for the pale ones.

Dots can be done with the tip of a paint brush, again dipped
in a strongly pigmented, thinly mixed paint. Stippling can be
achieved with a splayed paint brush, dotting it onto the painted
ground colour. Other effects can be imitated by stippling dry
powder pigment onto a painted surface which has been allowed
to set partially but not to dry out. The trick is to catch the surface at just the right point of dryness. If the pigment is stippled
onto the paint too soon, the surface will be disturbed. If too dry,
the pigment will not adhere. After application of the pigment,
bake, or air dry, the object, whichever is appropriate. This is
especially good for colouring cheeks, but allowance must be
made for the addition of a layer of glaze in calculating the depth
of colour to be applied.

11. Gilding

Matching gold leaf and bronze lustres is one of the most difficult problems facing the restorer. Probably the easiest to match is the soft yellow gold to be found on English soft-paste porcelain. Lustre wares are extremely difficult to imitate—the colours, the fine texture and the gloss all combine to present the restorer with one of his most perplexing tasks. For the first exercise in gilding, choose a small area without intricate detail.

Gold leaf The gold leaf must have a material to act as a size, to make it adhere to the object. The glaze medium which was used as the vehicle for the pigments, whether Chintex clear glaze, Chinaglaze or Bedacryl (Acryloid B48N) ought to work satisfactorily. The glaze medium must be tinted with a pigment so that it will be visible when the design is painted onto the surface—red is the most suitable for this purpose. The glaze must be fairly thin so that it will lie close to the surface and allow the gold leaf to do the same. Use a fine sable brush and paint the design onto the painted area, keeping it a little smaller than the original, and just overlapping at each end. This must then be allowed to become barely 'tacky' to the knuckle, and the time this takes will vary with the glaze medium used and the temperature and humidity. While the glaze medium is drying to the required stage, cut out the design in gold leaf. Do this very carefully with a small pair of very sharp scissors. A blunt pair will leave ragged edges on the leaf, which is to be avoided. One of the most difficult things to achieve is a clean-cut edge to the laid gold leaf. As soon as the glaze feels *just* tacky to the knuckle lay the cut-out gold leaf gently over the glaze. It will probably not fit exactly but don't worry. Carefully rub the back of the tissue with a finger or a boxwood modelling tool, or even

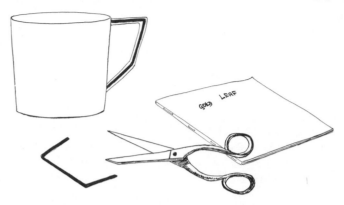

Fig. 16. Gold leaf must be cut to the required shape with very sharp scissors

an India rubber. Now, very gently lift the tissue away from the gold. What *should* be revealed is a neatly laid design in smooth gold leaf. Alas, this may not be the case! At the first try it will not be surprising if ragged edges, and patches where the gold has not adhered, meet the restorer's eye. Do not despair. There are remedies. First, with a very soft brush (the small ones used by photographers are excellent) dust off the little pieces of loose gold leaf which are giving the design the ragged look. If there are some very persistent pieces, use an orange stick gently, to push and coax the remaining pieces. The orange stick should be cut to a wedge shape and, believe it or not, wetted with spittle. Work as quickly as possible because a second layer must be laid over the first without adding a further layer of glaze at this stage. Again, cut out the design in gold leaf and lay it over the first, rubbing the back of the tissue as before. When the tissue is removed this time a more satisfactory sight should meet the eyes. There should only be a few very small pieces of gold leaf to be removed with the brush. If the leaf still does not look right, a second application of glaze will have to be painted over the design. Keep it as thin as possible because the two layers of glaze will tend to give a raised look, which, except in rare cases, is not required. Once the gold leaf has been brought as near the quality of the original as possible, the piece must be either baked, if Chintex was used, or left to air dry if China-glaze Clear Gloss was used instead. Bedacryl 122X (Acryloid B48N) has not been mentioned in this context as it is not very satisfactory as a size for gold leaf. However, the type of wares for which this glaze medium is suitable are unlikely to require gilding.

When the glaze beneath the gold leaf is absolutely dry, *and not before*, the gold is ready for burnishing. The agate burnisher can be worked directly onto the leaf, or it can be used over a piece of celluloid which can be bought at craft and model shops. Work the burnisher gently round and round until the desired depth of lustre has been reached.

If the area to be gilded is on a piece of porcelain which has had a great deal of wear the gold leaf will probably be thin and patchy and this condition must be copied. A layer of smooth shiny leaf without gaps would look out of place, and show up as an obvious repair. By using the tip of a finger, or a rubber, the edges of the gold can be made to look rubbed before application. Lightly stipple on the glaze medium where it reaches the edge of the design instead of laying it smoothly. When the leaf is laid it should look worn, to match the original. Sometimes further action will be required to make it look even more worn. A little powder pigment can be gently rubbed onto the leaf to darken it, but this must be done with extreme care.

To measure the amount of gold leaf which will be required for gilding straight lines, measure the width of the lines on the object with dividers, and mark it off very gently onto the gold leaf, or onto the piece of tissue which extends beyond the leaf.

Tablet gold Tablet gold should be reserved for very small sections because it is very expensive and rather extravagant to use. The minute tablet consists of gold bound with gum arabic. It must be applied with a very fine brush. Dip the tip of the little finger in cold water and just touch the top of the tablet with the drop, which will then leave the finger and rest on the gold. This seems to be the simplest way to transfer the smallest possible amount of water to the gold without swamping it or removing any of the gold. With the tip of the brush gently work the water into the gold until a certain amount has adhered to the brush. Now dab, rather than paint, the gold onto the area. The surface will look unpromising until it has been burnished. This must not be done until the gum arabic, which binds the gold, has been allowed to dry—about an hour should suffice. Test the gold with the tip of a finger and if no gold comes off it is ready for burnishing. Burnish over a piece of celluloid or directly onto the gold. A second application may be necessary. The finished result will be rich and glossy, but the surface will not be as tough as the gold leaf applied over glaze medium. If it is thought that the surface needs protecting, a thin coat of glaze may be painted over either gold leaf or tablet gold but this will probably alter the look of the gold. Chintex clear glaze, painted over gold leaf and then baked as usual will give the gold protection from a certain amount of use on everyday wares.

Bronze powders The only alternative to the above methods is to use bronze powders to *simulate* gold. These must be mixed with whichever glaze is being used for the rest of the painting, and painted on with a brush. If coated with a final layer of unpigmented glaze the bronze powders will last reasonably well. Their drawback is that they oxidize and discolour if not protected from the atmosphere. The smooth, polished look of pure gold can never be imitated by using bronze powders.

Lustre wares The restorer will have to use his ingenuity to conquer the problems facing him when he has to restore lustre wares, of whatever colour. No precise answer has yet been found. Spraying a tinted glaze over a layer of gold or silver leaf will sometimes answer, as will a tinted glaze over bronze powders, in very small areas. It is not advisable to take on lustre wares with large sections of repair—they will seldom look convincing when finished.

12. Surface finishing

Surface finishing means the polishing of a surface which is not sufficiently glossy, or the toning down of a too highly glossed surface. It is not always possible to achieve the correct surface with the painting process (although this is the most satisfactory way), and a little attention, once the final glaze is *absolutely dry*, will give the required finish. Solvol Autosol, applied with a soft, lint-free rag, will increase the gloss where the glazed surface is not quite shiny enough to match the surrounding glaze. Polish very gently, a little at a time, looking constantly to see that the gloss is not increased too much. It is always better to leave the repaired area slightly *less* glossy than the original glaze. Polishing will also help to blend the new surface with the old. A truly matt surface must be accomplished in the painting. It cannot be done by polishing. A surface which is only slightly too glossy however, can be polished to reduce the gloss. A good quality car polish, such as Simoniz, used on a damp rag, will gradually lessen the gloss. Again, care must be taken not to over-polish. Keep looking at the two surfaces, the original and the repaired, until they match as nearly as possible.

Ancient pottery which has a glaze with a dull look, but which is not actually matt, can often be matched by rubbing with a little of the dry clay, which is so often found inside them, over the restored area. Only a minute amount of the clay can be removed from the object and it must be done inconspicuously. By using the clay from the figure itself, the right colour will be used and it will be possible to blend the repair more easily with the original. This can also be done to merge a glazed area with an unglazed area and in each case can be carried out when the paint is still slightly damp. Since Bedacryl 122X (Acryloid B48N) will have been used on ancient pottery it will be fairly easy to catch the paint at the right moment.

Sometimes a slightly pitted look is needed. This can usually be imitated by placing a piece of fine sandpaper, face down, onto the dry paint surface, and rubbing the back gently with a boxwood modelling tool.

13. Restoring a porcelain pastille burner

Porcelain pastille burners in the shape of castles and cottages, and various animals, are much sought after by collectors for their quaint shapes and delicate colours. They make very decorative ornaments and are becoming increasingly difficult to find. The castle pictured has a pale lilac glaze, some gilding, and applied decoration in the form of pink and yellow flowers and clumps of pale green moss, and two tree trunks with a few leaves. The damage consisted of pieces inexpertly bonded back onto one of the turrets with some small chips missing. Several

7. Pastille burner showing extent of damage

of the flowers had new petals, and one or two leaves and some of the moss were missing. The old adhesive was epoxy resin, so the repairs were coated with Nitromors (methylene chloride) to break down the epoxy and to remove the added petals. Once the piece was thoroughly clean the sections of the turret were rebonded with Araldite AY 103 or Ablebond 342-1, then the pieces were strapped firmly into place with Scotch tape and left to set. Each flower is different and each had some petals remaining. This meant that although there were individual petals to use as patterns, there were no complete flowers from which to make moulds. It was decided to make some of the petals by the direct modelling method, with a firm Araldite or Ablebond 342-1 composition. Tiny moulds were then made with rubber latex of some of the other petals, and the leaves. Each restorer would approach this question from a different angle, considering time, ease of working procedure and his own personal preferences. Three layers of rubber latex were required for the petals but no thickening of the rubber was needed for such small objects. A hole was drilled in the stub of the branch which was to be built up by modelling, and a brass pin was cut to the right length, curved slightly and the surface roughened, before being set in composition and allowed to dry. Araldite AY 103 or Ablebond 342–1 was then well mixed to a thin composition with titanium dioxide and kaolin, and a minute amount was used to line the inside of the moulds (which had been dusted with talc) to ensure a smooth surface. The rest of the composition was thickened with further additions of titanium dioxide and kaolin to form a moderately firm mixture. Some of this mixture was tinted very pale lilac and the tiny chips near the joins on the turret were filled in, as were the joins themselves. Next, a small amount of marble flour (marble powder) was added to the main mixture and the moulds were filled, taking care not to push them out of shape. Quite a lot of marble flour (marble powder) was added to the lilac mixture and the piece of branch was built up over the pin, in two stages, the second stage being added the following day. Some of the white composition was thickened even more with kaolin to

8. The turret bonded and filled
and a new clump of moss

9. Composition branch and
leaf-tips

10. *Hand*-modelled petals

11. *Moulded* petals. Note
Plasticine props and tape

bring it to a stiff putty which could be rolled out on the piece of
plate glass. Petals were cut with a sharp blade, slightly
moistened with methylated spirits (ethyl alcohol). They were

left to harden until they could be bent and modelled without losing their shape, and tapered to a short stalk to enable them to be attached to the rest of the flower. A small amount of thin Araldite or Ablebond 342-1 composition was then mixed and applied to the flowers where the modelled petals were to be placed. The stalks of the petals were pressed into position over the thin composition and were supported with tiny pads of Plasticine (Roma Plastelina) dusted with talc. When the moulded foliage was dry it was checked for shape, sanded a little round the edges, and bonded into position.

The moss required rather special treatment so some of the firm composition was moulded to the approximate shape of each clump. They were then bonded into position with a little of the thin mixture. Using a light touch the composition was snipped, teased and poked, to make it look like stringy little clumps of moss. The tools used were a pair of very fine, pointed scissors, a pair of fine tweezers and a needle, all dipped in methylated spirits (ethyl alcohol). It is small, taxing jobs such as this that make porcelain restoring so fascinating and rewarding. The clumps of moss could have been made by the moulding process, but the results would not have been as satisfactory because much of the definition would have been lost.

To recapitulate, the pieces have been bonded onto the turret, new petals, leaves and moss have been made and bonded into place, and the missing branch has been modelled. Each section is now at the same stage, in need of sanding and preparing for painting. Each new piece was checked for pin holes and excess composition, and accuracy of surface. Excess composition round the joins was filed away and sanded smooth, and any holes were filled in. The surface of some of the petals and leaves was improved with gravers, fine sandpaper and needle files, and the chips along the joins on the turret were sanded, care being taken not to scratch the glaze.

Everything was now ready for painting by hand. A white paint was then mixed, using Chinaglaze Clear Gloss and titanium dioxide white pigment and a small amount of Phenthin 83. This was tested to make sure that there was sufficient white pigment to disguise the repairs and each piece of composition was then painted carefully, just covering the joins, and the joins on the turret painted, keeping the area of paint to the absolute minimum. No coloured pigments were added to the white because the white body of the porcelain is seen through the coloured glazes and it would not have been possible to imitate this effect if colours had been added to the first layer of paint. This point should be borne in mind when painting porcelain. The paint was *stippled* onto the moss to prevent the gaps being filled with paint and the stringy effect being destroyed. The castle was set aside for two days before starting with the largest area—the turret, and the branch in the same colour. The pale lilac was mixed by combining a small amount of white with French ultramarine and alizarin crimson. The paint was applied sparingly and edges carefully faded onto the glaze. The petals were painted next, with a pale mixture of aureolin yellow and a very little white. The minimum number

12. Painting in progress

of brush strokes were employed to avoid build-ups of paint on such a limited area. The paint was carried underneath the petals and neatly faded out onto the stalks. A pale green mixture, consisting of a little white, and French ultramarine and aureolin yellow, was painted onto the leaves and stippled onto the moss.

Again, the castle was allowed to dry for forty-eight hours. With the third layer of paint each section was brought to its correct colour. No white was used in either of the mixtures in this round, except for a minute amount in the pink for the petals. French ultramarine and aureolin yellow were mixed with a touch of burnt sienna to make the correct shade of green for the leaves. At the same time a separate mixing of burnt sienna was made. The green was painted onto the leaves,

13. The castle completed

leaving about a third free for the burnt sienna which was run
into the green. When the leaves were almost dry, some tiny lines
were painted onto the other colours, using a mixture of burnt
sienna and burnt umber. Returning to the petals, two shades of
pink were mixed, one using a *very* little white with alizarin
crimson, and the second using alizarin crimson and a little
burnt sienna, for the tips of the petals. The first mixture was
painted onto the middle third of the petals and the darker
mixture was painted onto the tips of the petals so that it ran into
the other pink. Some little dots and squiggles were painted on
with a mixture of French ultramarine, alizarin crimson and, for
some of them, a little burnt umber was added. The moss was
stippled with some of the green which was used for the leaves. It
only remained to apply a coat of tinted glaze using small amounts
of French ultramarine and alizarin crimson, to the turret and the
branch. This was followed by a coat of plain glaze.

14. Restoring a Chelsea plate

The plate had part of the openwork rim missing and the glaze was worn and discoloured in the centre. The ground colour is off-white with a blue-green glaze, which lies in pools in some places. It is decorated in green, yellow and a red which varies from magenta to almost brown. The first stage was to clean the plate to remove as much dirt as possible from the badly rubbed areas. Washing in Synperonic NDB (Triton X100) and de-ionized (demineralized) water did not seem to remove completely the dirt which had settled firmly into the rough surface

14. Chelsea plate with missing flower and piece out of rim. Note very dirty glaze

of some of the glaze. Swabs of cotton wool, dipped in a bleaching solution—one part hydrogen peroxide 100 vol. (hydrogen peroxide 30–35%), three parts de-ionized (demineralized) water, a few drops ammonia 880 (ammonia 28%) (see pages 31 and 41)—were laid over these areas, covered with clear plastic and left for about two hours. This process was repeated several times with fresh swabs. While the rubbed areas will always remain, because it is not acceptable to paint glaze over extended areas, the dirt was removed successfully, and the appearance of the plate was improved beyond recognition. The colours became brighter and the surface of the glaze, on most of the plate, glossier. The next stage was to decide how to restore the missing piece on the rim. There is a certain amount of detail because of the raised flowers, so it was decided to use a rubber latex moulding material which would pick up the detail and be easy to remove. No dowel or pin was required in the rather small enclosed area. To prevent the latex from escaping through the hole, a piece of tape was placed beneath the area on which the mould was to be made. A coat of rubber latex was then painted over the chosen section, and slightly beyond, and extended over the rim to the other side of the plate by about 0·625 cm ($\frac{1}{4}$ in). The latex was allowed to fill the hole. By extending the mould to an area larger than that of the broken piece the correct location of the mould over the damaged area was ensured. The first layer of latex was allowed to dry until the next day when it had turned from a creamy colour and texture to a pale brown rubber. Some latex was then mixed with minute snippets of cotton wool to strengthen the mixture and reduce the number of layers, and was applied to the dry first coat as evenly as possible. Another coat of the thickened latex was applied as soon as the second one had dried. The plate was set aside once more for the mould to dry. Then it was time to remove the mould by very gently turning it back over the rim and peeling it off. It was dusted with talc to prevent the filling from sticking to the rubber.

The mould was slipped over the missing section to make sure that the fit was correct. It was then removed.

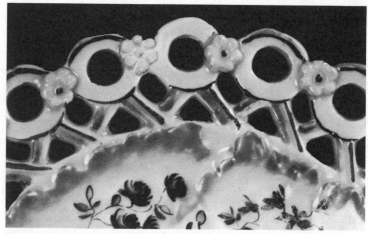

15. The plate has been cleaned and the damaged area filled in

The composition was mixed by adding titanium dioxide powder to either Araldite AY 103 or Ablebond 342-1 and Hardener HY 956. Some kaolin powder and a very little marble flour (marble powder) were added to form a moderately firm mixture. Before filling, the mould was coated with a *thin* layer of soft Araldite or Ablebond 342-1 composition in order that the surface of the dry cast would be smooth, which would not be the case if the firm composition were put directly into the moulds. Some of the soft composition was also applied to the edges of the porcelain to provide good adhesion for the cast.

The mould was filled with the composition which was pressed into the extremities to expel the air and prevent the formation of bubbles. The surface was smoothed over, using a tool moistened with methylated spirits (ethyl alcohol). The mould was then put in place on the rim of the plate and taped firmly with Scotch tape. The plate was propped, upside down, with Plasticine (Roma Plastelina), so that the exposed surface of the filling was exactly horizontal, and left to dry until the next day. The mould was removed, revealing a cast of the missing piece firmly bonded into place, and needing only a little attention. The surface of the cast needed some filing and sanding where it joined the porcelain, some sharpening of the detail with a graver, and a little more sanding. The underneath of the cast piece had to be sanded slightly to reduce the level to that of the plate, and the same attention was given to the joins as was carried out on the upper surface. The whole area was cleaned with acetone to remove dust and finger marks before painting, and then polished with Solvol Autosol.

Chinaglaze Clear Gloss was selected as the most suitable glaze medium for this plate. A piece of this age would not be suitable for baking, and, as it is soft-paste porcelain, baking might easily damage it. This cancelled out Chintex as the medium. Given the painting skill of the experienced restorer, Bedacryl 122X (Acryloid B48N) would also have been suitable. In this instance Chinaglaze Clear Gloss was mixed with Phenthin 83 and white pigment to provide an opaque paint which would cover the repair in the first layer. Trace amounts of viridian green, yellow ochre and burnt umber were also added to bring the first layer a little nearer to the colour of

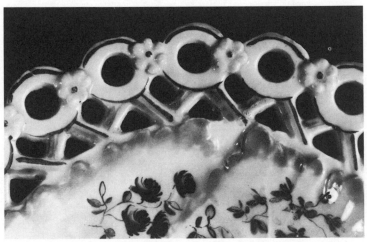

16. The finished plate. Note how the style of painting matches the original

the plate. This was painted over the repair and faded out *just* beyond the join. It was almost invisible, so the remaining layers would stand a good chance of being completely so. The piece was then set aside to dry before sanding. Since the first layer of paint had proved successful, the second needed *very* little white, but some more coloured pigment was added.

A first layer of decoration in the form of aureolin yellow and white for the flower, white, viridian green and burnt umber for the green lines, and alizarin crimson, French ultramarine and burnt umber for the dark red lines was painted as soon as the second layer was dry. This was also allowed to dry before a coat of tinted glaze was painted over the decoration. The flower, the green lines and the magenta lines were brought to the correct colour by the addition of the same colours as before, but without any white. When these had dried, the plate was given a final coat of clear glaze over the repaired areas.

15. Restoring a Derby vase

The vase is white with black and gold decoration and a panel of polychrome flowers. The body of the vase was in excellent condition, but both handles were missing. No vase with identical handles was available so a handle had to be modelled from a photograph and a two-piece mould made on the modelled handle. This is a difficult procedure for the beginner, but, since this problem will frequently arise it is dealt with here. A piece of modelling wax was rolled to the approximate length of the handle and then curved to shape. A piece of wire was pushed into it to give it solidity for handling. It was modelled and carved using modelling tools, with constant reference to both the photograph and the vase. Work of this nature is exacting and it would be wise to do a little at a time. A line was then drawn down the centre of the handle on top *and* underneath. This was the separation line for the two sections of the mould. Since there were no under-cuts and large, firm moulds were required, it was decided to use a silicone rubber moulding material. A Plasticine (Roma Plastelina) wall was built so as to leave half of the handle exposed lengthwise. To explain further, the handle was embedded in a large, flat piece of Plasticine (Roma Plastelina) up to the level of the pencil line. More Plasticine (Roma Plastelina) was rolled out and cut into a long flat piece about an inch wide, which was then stood on the other piece of Plasticine (Roma Plastelina), leaving about 2 cm ($\frac{3}{4}$ in) on either side of the handle. The wall was sealed to the Plasticine (Roma Plastelina) floor by making small diagonal cuts across the join which were then smoothed over, creating a surface through which the rubber could not escape. Shallow holes were cut into the floor near the outer edge, to make keys to provide for accurate mating of the two halves of the mould. The

17. Derby vase with handles missing

silicone rubber was mixed and poured into the prepared Plasticine (Roma Plastelina) 'box', taking care to pour slowly from one end of the handle and allowing the rubber to flow across the handle, pushing the air before it. This was done to avoid the formation of air bubbles which happens all too easily with this type of material. The moulding material was allowed almost to fill the box, approximately twice the depth of the exposed part of the handle, and was then left to set until the next day. The mould was not removed from the handle because it was to serve as the floor of the second half of the mould. The Plasticine (Roma Plastelina) was removed from the bottom and sides of the rubber. The surface of the rubber had to be coated with Slipwax release agent (Butcher's Wax) to ensure that the two halves of the mould would not stick together, but avoiding the handle.

A new wall now had to be built to contain the second half of the mould, placing the Plasticine (Roma Plastelina) round the rubber and extending it above by about 2·5 cm (1 in). A second batch of rubber was mixed, poured, and left to dry. Then the box was removed and the two halves of the mould separated and put into a 65°C (150°F) oven for one hour to dry. When cool

18. Composition handle lying in one half of the silicone rubber mould. Note keys

they were dusted out with talc and coated with a thin mixture of Araldite or Ablebond 342-1 composition. The mould was then filled with a firm composition containing titanium dioxide, kaolin and a little marble flour (marble powder). The *edges* of the rubber were smeared with more release agent to ensure easy separation of the two halves, *avoiding the filling*. The two moulds were brought together, matching the keys, bound with electrical wire, and left for at least twenty-four hours. Upon separation of the mould halves, a reasonable copy of a handle emerged, but it required a certain amount of sanding, pointing with gravers, and an addition of some more composition to improve the shape which was not quite accurate in some small details. A second handle was made, using the same moulds. Dowels were made from stainless steel wire and slightly curved to match the shape of the handle. The wire was roughened with a file to provide a better hold for the adhesive. 16 gauge wire was chosen as being the best size for the handles, the stubs of which are $1 \cdot 41$ cm ($\frac{9}{16}$ in) $\times 0 \cdot 78$ cm ($\frac{5}{16}$ in) but owing to the *shape* the hole could not be more than about $0 \cdot 47$ cm ($\frac{3}{16}$ in) in diameter. The holes in the stubs and the handles were drilled to the depth of a generous $1 \cdot 41$ cm ($\frac{9}{16}$ in), this being three times the diameter of the wire. Then a thin Araldite or Ablebond 342-1 composition was worked into the holes *in the handles only*. The dowels were pushed into the holes slowly, expelling any air, and the excess composition. The handles were fitted to the vase to ensure correct alignment, some kaolin having been previously dusted onto the *porcelain stubs* to prevent bonding at this stage. The handles were strapped in place and left until the *dowel* adhesive had set. Next, the handle was removed and a thin composition was pushed into the holes in the vase and more was applied to the stubs. The handles were again fitted into position, this time permanently. They were Scotch-taped to prevent movement, and left until the following day. The joins were sanded and any small gaps were filled and sanded again.

The new handles were now ready for painting. Again, the Chinaglaze Clear Gloss was decided upon as being the most suitable glaze medium, but Bedacryl 122X (Acryloid B48N) could have been used. This time it was sprayed on to ensure even dispersion over the entire surface of both handles. Several layers were required to bring the surfaces to the quality of the original. The white was lessened as the work proceeded and a little yellow ochre was introduced into the final glaze. Black with a little burnt umber was painted onto the stubs at the top of the handles, matching the black glaze where it met the handles. Next, the long task of applying the gold leaf was started. Two, and in some places three, layers of gold were needed to match the rich gold of the original leaf. Finally the gold was burnished and the vase was complete—a long and arduous piece of restoration but well worth the time spent.

19. One of the new handles in place

20. Painted and gilded—a completed handle

16. Restoring a Creamware centrepiece

This piece of Creamware had been repaired before but the added sections had broken off and been lost, and the remaining paint had discoloured badly. The first procedure was to remove all traces of the old repair, followed by the cleaning of the whole object. The paint was easily removed with acetone-soaked swabs. The broken edges were wetted with de-ionized (demineralized) water, and swabs of Nitromors (methylene chloride) were applied to remove traces of shellac. They were then bleached by the hydrogen peroxide method (see pages 31 and 41), to try and lighten them. They did not come absolutely clean. Swabs soaked in the solution were also laid over some

21. The upper section of the Creamware centrepiece showing missing areas

worn areas which had become ingrained with dirt. After three applications these were gradually improved.

The next step was to prepare a mould. This involved painting a layer of rubber latex onto two of the original petal-shaped sections, noting the extent of the missing areas and allowing for about 0·625 cm ($\frac{1}{4}$ in) of overlap on each side, and along the bottom of the mould. It was decided to use a rubber latex rather than a silicone rubber moulding material because the rubber latex is more flexible and easier to remove from the rather fragile petal shapes. The first layer of rubber was painted onto the clean dry surface of the ceramic, using care to avoid bubbles, and allowed to dry completely. A second layer was painted over the first and, when it was dry, a third layer, thickened with small snippets of butter muslin or cheese-cloth well mixed into the rubber. Next, a supporting mould of plaster of Paris was made over the rubber mould, with a thin coating of Slipwax release agent (Butcher's Wax) was smeared onto the rubber to help separate the two moulds. The plaster was

22. The rubber latex mould in position with the plaster support over it

allowed to dry thoroughly and then gently eased off the rubber, using a gentle rocking movement to work it up and away without breaking either the plaster or the ceramic. The rubber mould was removed and placed back in its plaster support or 'mother'. The two were then fitted onto the ceramic over the broken edges of the missing petals. Scotch tape was used to secure the mould and its support and ensure that they would not move at the crucial moment when the filling was added. The inside of the mould was dusted with talc making sure that no excess was left in the tips of the petals. A thin filling mixture, consisting of Araldite AY 103 and Hardener HY 956 or Ablebond 342-1 mixed with kaolin powder, titanium dioxide and aureolin yellow (a very small amount of the latter), was worked into the mould with a boxwood tool. The filling was thickened by the addition of further quantities of kaolin but was kept soft enough to be worked easily into the mould without having to use force and so disturb the position of the mould. The centrepiece was set aside until the next day to allow the filling to dry. The plaster support was removed, followed by the rubber mould. The petals needed a certain amount of sanding to bring the inside surface level with the glaze. The grooves in the outside surface were sharpened with gravers and needle files, and the area where the filling joined the ceramic was sanded, and a few discrepancies both inside and outside were filled in with composition, mixed as before. These were also sanded when dry.

With the new petals ready for painting, Bedacryl 122X (Acryloid B48N) was mixed with titanium dioxide, Cellosolve (acetate) solvent and Xylene (approximately 50 per cent of each), a touch of aureolin yellow and burnt sienna, and some matting agent. This mixture was painted over the restored area and extended just beyond to ensure the disguise of the dark lines where the composition joined the ceramic. (These lines were caused by the burning of the ceramic when the previous restorer used heat to melt shellac, and a shadow remained.) The edges of the overpainting were gently faded out onto the surface of the glaze, using a fine brush.

23. The composition petals almost ready for painting

After two days the paint was dry enough to take a second layer, containing considerably less white pigment, only a little aureolin yellow, and no burnt umber. This was again left to dry for about two days when a final layer of clear glaze with just a suspicion of aureolin yellow, was laid over the painted area.

24. The painted and finished centrepiece

The painting process with a piece such as this is comparatively simple in that there was no pattern or design to think of. The only things which had to be watched were the fading of the edges onto the glaze, and care had to be taken to ensure that the paint did not fill the grooves on the outside of the petals. This was done by *stippling* the paint into the grooves and making sure that the paint did not collect in pools.

After a further period of drying to allow the surface to harden, it was polished very gently with Simoniz car polish to lessen the gloss so that it would blend with the ceramic glaze.

17. Restoring a tin-glazed earthenware cup

This small two-handled cup was badly cracked and two pieces had been bonded inaccurately, leaving raised edges which had become very dirty. The cracks were discoloured, as were the areas of exposed pottery on the rim of the cup. Two chips were missing and the gaps badly in need of cleaning. The first step was to soak the object in acetone to separate the bonded pieces. By good fortune the old adhesive responded to the acetone after an hour's soaking. Once the pieces had been separated they were left in fresh acetone for a little longer to make sure that the remaining adhesive dissolved from the edges, and brushing with a soft bristle brush and more acetone finished the cleaning work. The pieces were now ready for the bleaching process. A

25. Tin-glazed earthenware cup showing old repairs and the dirty cracks

26. Bleaching the edges after separation and cleaning

hydrogen peroxide solution (one part hydrogen peroxide, three parts water, a few drops of ammonia (see pages 31 and 41) was prepared, and the pieces of pottery were soaked in de-ionized (demineralized) water. Swabs of cotton wool dipped in the solution were then laid over the whole area of the pottery. The pieces were put into a plastic bowl and the bowl was covered with kitchen foil. After about two hours they were inspected and found to be very much improved in appearance. However, it was decided that further bleaching would improve them even more, so fresh swabs were prepared and laid on the pottery. A third application was necessary to complete the removal of all the dirt and discoloration. The pieces were laid aside to dry before a final cleaning with acetone. The edges of the two loose pieces were wetted with de-ionized (demineralized) water, then bonded, using polyvinyl acetate emulsion P.V.A. They were taped, and propped with the join lying in a horizontal position, to allow the adhesive to dry. After twenty-four hours the joined sections were set into the cup after further wetting and application of P.V.A.

27. The filled in chips and cracks

Next, the chips had to be filled in. It was decided to use plaster of Paris with P.V.A., a little kaolin and water, with the addition of powder pigments, yellow ochre and burnt umber, to match the buff-coloured pottery. The surface of the filling was gently smoothed with water and left to dry. It only required a minimal amount of sanding to bring the surface level with the surrounding glaze. The ground colour, as is usually the case with tin-glazed earthenware, has a pink tinge, caused by the clay showing through the glaze. The decoration is under-glaze blue and the surface of the glaze is glossy. Bedacryl 122X (Acryloid B48N) was used as the glaze medium and was mixed with Xylene and Cellosolve solvent to a manageable consistency for hand painting. A fairly high percentage of white pigment was added as well as burnt sienna and a little burnt umber. It was decided to leave the rim free of paint because it would have meant covering far too large an area of so small a piece, and the absence of glaze on the rim had been caused by normal wear through the years. So the *two chips* and the *joins* were coloured, *but the cracks which had been bleached were left free of paint*. This first layer was left to dry for two days before starting to apply the blue decoration. The blue was mixed by adding ultramarine blue and a small amount of burnt sienna and burnt umber to a glaze mixture containing a little white. The addition of red was avoided because it turns the blue almost purple in some lights. The patches of blue were put on with a small brush, keeping them a little smaller than the original, and making the edges blurred rather than sharp-edged. This was allowed to dry for twenty-four hours and then sanded, making sure that the surface was even. The blue was then traced over with a darker mixture, containing no white, which brought it to the correct tone. After a further twenty-four hours a glaze faintly tinted with burnt sienna was laid over the whole area, and the edges were carefully faded onto the surrounding glaze. This was allowed to dry thoroughly for two days. It was then inspected for accuracy of colour and surface. The glaze did not appear to have quite enough depth so a second, thin, untinted glaze was laid over the first and this gave an improved gloss.

28. The finished cup painted to match the surrounding area

18. A word on restoring T'ang pottery

T'ang pottery is as popular as ever with collectors but the buyer who finds a piece of T'ang without any restoration or repair is fortunate indeed. Genuine pieces can be found with very little repair but the restorer will almost invariably have to clean away old work before the new restoration can begin.

Repairs on T'ang pottery can usually be removed with acetone. Lay swabs of cotton wool dipped in acetone over the repaired areas, changing them frequently, because acetone evaporates. Evaporation can be delayed by placing the object in a large plastic bowl and covering it with kitchen foil. If absolutely necessary the object may be soaked in acetone. Keep as much of it as possible out of the acetone by propping it in the receptacle with a plastic box, or it can be suspended over the bowl in a sling made out of clean white rag. Pour in the acetone, just covering the old repair, or drape a long piece of cotton wool over the repair, dipping both ends in the solvent. Most T'ang pottery has a certain amount of dried clay chiefly inside the body, collected when the piece was buried for hundreds of years. This should *not* be removed because it is part of its history. If the old repairs do not respond to acetone, use Nitromors (methylene chloride). To prevent this from penetrating the pottery and drawing the dissolved paint and glue with it, first soak in water, then, when the Nitromors (methylene chloride) is applied, it will remain on the surface, without drawing the old paint into the ceramic. For the removal of the paint apply swabs dipped in Nitromors (methylene chloride) to the surface of the old repairs and place the object in the covered container for about an hour. Remove the swabs and repeat, if necessary, several times, until the paint has softened. To break down the old adhesive with Nitromors (methylene chloride), first wet the areas on either side of the join with water, but do not allow the water to flow into the inside of the object and so dislodge the clay. After about ten minutes, when the pottery will have absorbed a certain amount of water, apply the Nitromors (methylene chloride) swabs to the joins, place the object again in the container and leave for approximately another hour. The times for leaving the Nitromors (methylene chloride) swabs in place will vary with the type of paint and adhesive to be removed and the restorer will learn with experience how long to wait before changing the swabs. *Do not attempt to force the joins apart* because chunks of glaze and pottery will break away with the adhesive, if it has not been softened fully by the Nitromors (methylene chloride). When the joins will part without force remove all the swabs and apply fresh ones to each side of the parted joins to remove the adhesive. This could take several more applications. It may be necessary to use a fine-pointed scalpel blade to lift gently away any remaining pieces of adhesive. Clean the whole area with acetone to de-grease. Keep all the pieces together on a lined tray. If there are many pieces, including small chips, it would be advisable to put the latter into a small box with a lid, but keep them with the larger pieces. It is also a good idea to make a note of the total number of pieces, including the main section.

Polyvinyl acetate emulsion (P.V.A.) is the adhesive to use. Decide on the order of bonding and then damp the edges with a brush dipped in water, or apply swabs. Spread a thin layer of P.V.A. onto one edge only of each join to within 0.31 cm ($\frac{1}{8}$ in) of the end. Bring the pieces together very gently and *without* the rocking movement used to ascertain the correct position when bonding porcelain. With coarse-grained pottery it is fairly easy to find the key and then gently but firmly press the edges together. Strap the sections with Scotch tape and stand in the sand box, or prop in a pad of Plasticine (Roma Plastelina). Continue until the object is in one piece.

The filling for the cracks and for building up any missing pieces can be either Polyfilla, or plaster of Paris combined with water, a little kaolin and P.V.A., and both can have pigments

added to match, as near as possible, the honey-coloured
pottery. A combination of yellow ochre, burnt umber and a
little light red will probably give the right colour. For filling
cracks and chips use the plaster or Polyfilla in small quantities.
Both Polyfilla and plaster of Paris can be smoothed into place
with a spatula, or a boxwood modelling tool dipped in water,
but be careful not to flood the surface. Once the filling is dry,
gentle sanding is used to level the surface with the surrounding
glaze, but great caution is advised because the glaze is *very*
easily scratched. If the surface of a filling made with Polyfilla is
not satisfactory, a layer of Fine Surface Polyfilla, tinted to
match the other layer, is applied carefully so that no further
sanding should be necessary. Owing to the crazing of the glaze
the colour-matching is extremely difficult. The chestnut glaze
can vary from a deep yellow-green to one with a certain amount
of blue in it where the glaze has run into the chestnut. Some of
this pottery has a *wonderful* blue glaze and it can also be found
with deep brown splashes running into a pale cream ground.
The surfaces can range from very highly glazed to a matt
surface. The chestnut glazes can be achieved by varying
mixtures of raw sienna, burnt sienna, aureolin yellow, raw
umber or burnt umber, and sometimes Indian red. For the
greens, viridian combined with aureolin, raw or burnt umber,
French ultramarine. These have been found successful, but
again the restorer will come to his own conclusions as to the best
way to reach the colour he wants. Keep all the colours on the
light side because mixtures that are too dark will show far more
than ones that are too light.

Reinforcement is necessary where a large piece is missing,
such as a tail, or where part of a leg has a poor key to the rest of
the leg because of wear caused by bad previous repair, missing
chips, or a difficult angle. Most owners would rather not have a
new tail or for that matter other extensive additions, and this is
the case with museum pieces. If an original tail suffers from the
same problems in relation to the body (as the above-mentioned
leg section had in relation to the rest of the leg), it will need
reinforcement to provide a sufficiently strong bond. Another

instance where reinforcement might be required is for the base of a very heavy T'ang horse or camel, and it would be advisable to join the pieces with dowels. Heads are inclined to be top-heavy and have large cavities inside, especially on large horses, and it is recommended that a tube dowel (a piece of fine gauge sheet brass made into a roll) be bonded into place, leaving the area inside the dowel hollow.

Owing to the refraction of light in the glaze it will be found that with some colours the application of the paint will create a dark shadow where it overlaps the glaze. This can be avoided by keeping the paint within the confines of the repaired area. In many cases the repair will be visible, but, as long as the work is neat, this is infinitely preferable to hiding the original glaze under layers of paint. The application of the colour is best achieved by stippling with a fine brush and using a thin mixture with plenty of pigment. The first layer of Bedacryl 122X (Acryloid B48N) with Xylene and Cellosolve will have to contain *some* white but this should be kept to a minimum. Where the colours blend into each other, soften the edges of the paint with some plain glaze medium, thinned with Xylene or this can be done with a small amount of Xylene alone. Where the glaze has been 'splashed' on and there are long trickles running from the shoulder of a horse down its legs, instead of painting in the direction of the trickle, work the colour upwards and this will, surprisingly, create a more natural reproduction.

Airbrushing should not be used on ancient pottery because of the overspray, which would cover areas of original glaze. It should not be used on unglazed pottery unless there is a very large repaired area to be disguised.

Careful sanding between each layer of colour will give a smooth surface. There are so many variations to the pottery theme that it would be impossible to cover them all here, but by following these hints, making notes while working, and remembering that the more of the original that is left visible, the better, the restorer will soon be able to achieve successful restoration on T'ang and other ancient pottery. Any doubts as to the best type of restoration to use on a given piece should be referred, if possible, to a museum conservation officer for advice.

Caution: To remove Scotch tape from pottery without dislodging pieces of glaze, dip a small, soft brush in acetone, lift one corner of the tape with the tip of a blade, then push the tape gently off the pottery with the brush. Use as little acetone as possible. *Never* rip tape off—it can cause untold damage.

19. Porcelain dolls' heads

Antique dolls can be repaired by the ceramics restorer. A severely damaged head means that the eye mechanism will have to be replaced correctly, and it would be wise to leave that work to a doll specialist.

The doll's clothes should be removed before beginning work and the body of the doll wrapped in plenty of tissue paper or plastic to protect it from damage and stray drops of paint. Most dolls' heads are made of unglazed porcelain with patches of bright colour on the cheeks.

The process of restoring a doll's head is much the same as for other porcelain. The pieces are thoroughly cleaned before carefully reassembling with Araldite AY and Hardener HY 956 or Ablebond 342-1 tinted to match the porcelain, but remember to keep it lighter than the original rather than darker. Once the head has been put together, chips, cracks, and missing pieces are filled in with either an Araldite or Ablebond 342-1 composition, also tinted to come as near as possible to the shade of the porcelain. When the filling has dried, the surfaces are sanded down to the level of the surrounding area and any small discrepancies made good and then sanded again. The painting will have to be done with the airbrush, except for the details, such as eyebrows, nostrils, and lips.

The first layer of ground colour will require plenty of white and matting agent (see page 33) to form an opaque paint which will disguise the repairs. It can be tinted with a very little Naples yellow, Payne's grey, and a touch of burnt sienna or cadmium red. It will be found that each doll varies in the colour of the porcelain, so careful testing will have to be carried out to determine which pigments produce the correct match. After the first layer of paint applied with the airbrush, use as little white as possible, leaving it out altogether in the final layer and keeping the number of layers to the minimum. Since the surface is matt, a matting agent will have to be used with each layer, and a point to remember is that a matt paint dries a little lighter than a glossy surface. Each layer must be very carefully and thoroughly sanded to produce the unblemished final surface. Cheeks are also sprayed on with the airbrush so that the colour will blend into the surrounding area. Again colours vary but rose madder genuine will often be found to match the cheek colour. If the final surface looks too bright, it can be toned down with a further layer of glaze containing a *very* little white. Used judiciously, this will give the right effect.

Eyebrows must be painted with a very fine brush, a oo series 7, using a thin, strong paint mixture, very little white with probably burnt sienna and burnt umber or black. Lips consist of varying combinations of cadmium red, Indian red and burnt sienna. Keep the outline of the lips just a little smaller than the original so that the fact that they have been painted will not be too obvious. This also applies to the eyebrows. A final layer of *untinted* matt glaze can be added to protect these areas.

Glossary

Adhesive Material used to bond sections of ceramic, and to bind the powders used in filling in and building up missing areas.

Air-drying Term applied to glaze mediums which dry on exposure to air as opposed to those which need baking.

Baking Drying a surface painted with a heat-drying glaze in the domestic oven.

Bonding Process of joining two pieces of ceramic with an adhesive.

Breaking down The dissolving of a previous repair with a solvent or paint stripper.

Building up The addition of composition to a piece of ceramic to replace a missing part.

Burnisher Tool used to burnish gold leaf. It consists of a polished agate stone set into a piece of metal at the end of a long handle.

Burnishing Method of polishing gold leaf after laying. An agate burnisher is worked gently over the surface of the gold to improve the gloss.

Cast The piece of composition which, when dry, is removed from the mould in the shape of the part to be replaced.

Cleaning Removal of dust, dirt, stains, and all forms of prior repair.

Colour-matching The mixing of powder pigments or oil colours to imitate the colours on ceramics.

Conservation The care and preservation of ceramics in the laboratories of the museums. The objects are cleaned, then restored as little as possible in order to preserve them as near to their original state as is compatible with their welfare.

Crackle Describes the *intentional* cracks in the glaze to be found on certain types of Chinese porcelain.

Crazing *Unintentional* cracks found in the surface of the glaze on some European porcelain.

Decoration Applies to any form of ornamentation or embellishment, whether overglaze or underglaze, applied or gilded.

Dowel Length of wire used to form a dowel.

Dowelling Process used to strengthen two sections of a heavy piece, or to join an arm to a body, etc.; wire is cut to fit, and set into drilled holes.

Drilling The preparatory operation in dowelling and pinning. Holes are drilled for the wire dowel, or pin, and filled with composition.

Feathering Otherwise known as fading. The process of gradually blending a painted edge with the surrounding area.

Filling in Method of making good chips, cracks and apertures.

Finishing Process of toning down or polishing final glaze surface to match surrounding glaze.

Fire crack Term used to describe cracks in the ceramic caused in the original firing. Not usually restored.

Gilding The application of gold leaf.

Glazing The final layer of glaze medium, sometimes containing a small amount of colour, applied over the layers of paint.

Glue A term usually applied to animal-based adhesives.

Keying The fitting together of two pieces of ceramic to form a perfect bond.

Locking out Term used in bonding when a piece will not fit into place because the previous two or more pieces have been put together in the wrong order.

Mending Repairing, restoring.

Modelling Freehand formation of new limbs for figures, and many other broken and missing parts.

Mother Another word for the plaster support made to fit onto the outside of rubber latex moulds to prevent them from bending and so losing their shape.

Overglaze decoration The decoration on ceramics which

was added after glazing and therefore required a separate firing.

Overspray The matt area round the edge of a coat of sprayed paint. If the airbrush has been correctly set it can be kept to a minimum.

Painting Overpainting, retouching. The disguise of the repair with colours bound in a glaze medium.

Pinning Describes a length of wire cut to size and set into a drilled hole in the stub of an arm, or other missing part.

Polishing The improvement of a surface. Solvol Autosol is used to prepare a dry composition surface for painting; various polishes are used to alter finished glaze surfaces.

Pressed mould Mould made by pressing a soft substance such as Plasticine (Roma Plastelina) or Paribar (Mercaptan-MIM) onto the area to be reproduced.

Pressing The result of a pressed mould.

Reinforcing Used to describe the process of strengthening joins with dowels or pins.

Repairing Mending, restoring.

Restoring As above.

Retouching Painting, overpainting.

Sand box Container with sand in which work in progress can be propped.

Sanding Process of rubbing down excess composition with sandpaper.

Separator A material used to prevent sections of moulds, etc. sticking to each other.

Solvent Liquids used to dissolve old paints, adhesives, etc., for instance, acetone for cellulose adhesives. Also the name for the thinner for a glaze medium, e.g. Phenthin 83 for Chinaglaze Clear Gloss.

Spraying Spray-painting or airbrushing. Process of painting a repaired area with an airbrush.

Sprung Used to describe a piece of broken porcelain, usually a curved section from the rim of a cup or bowl, which has warped and no longer fits into its original place.

Sticking Another term for bonding, but the latter usually preferred.

Stippling The application of the paint by dabbing the brush so that a speckled look is achieved.

Strapping The holding together of bonded sections with tape to prevent them falling apart before the adhesive has dried.

Support Either a plaster mother made to fit the outside of a rubber latex mould, which would otherwise not retain its shape, or a pad of Plasticine (Roma Plastelina) used to prop a bonded piece or to prop an object in any given position.

Swabbing The cleaning of a given area while work is in progress, using a rag, cotton wool or a small piece of tissue held in a pair of tweezers, dipped in the appropriate solvent.

Swabs Pieces of cotton wool dipped in a solvent and laid over a stained area, e.g. when using hydrogen peroxide, ammonia and water when bleaching.

Thickener The material—snippets of cotton wool or butter-muslin or cheese-cloth—which are mixed with rubber latex to strengthen the moulds.

Thinner The solvent used to dilute a given glaze medium.

Tinting The addition of very small amounts of colour in a coat of clear glaze.

Under-cut Space beneath a protruding piece of ceramic which would make the removal of moulds difficult.

Underglaze decoration The decoration on ceramics which was added before glazing and fired at the same time.

Reference books

Restoration and conservation

China Mending and Restoration
C. S. M. Parsons and F. H. Curl. Faber. 1963
  The first comprehensive book on ceramics repairing. Covers all aspects, including museum work and riveting. Many useful illustrations.

Restoring Ceramics
Judith Larney. Barrie and Jenkins. 1975
  A very welcome addition to the sparse list of books on the restoration of ceramics. The author is head of Ceramic Conservation and Restoration at the Victoria and Albert Museum and writes with the authority of one who has the resources of a long-established conservation laboratory at her disposal. Interesting illustrations.

The Conservation of Antiquities and Works of Art: treatment, repair and restoration
H. J. Plenderleith and Anthony Werner, revised edition. London. Oxford University Press. 1971
  For those interested in the type of repair carried out on archaeological finds. Dr. Plenderleith and Dr. Werner are world-renowned authorities on conservation.

British ceramics

Derby Porcelain
Franklin A. Barrett and Arthur L. Thorpe. Faber. 1971

Worcester Porcelain and Lund's Bristol
Franklin A. Barrett. Faber. 1966

New Hall and its Imitators
David Holgate. Faber. 1971

English Cream-coloured Earthenware
Donald Towner. Faber. 1957

English Delftware
F. H. Garner and Michael Archer. Faber. 1972 (New edition)

Mediaeval English Pottery
Bernard Rackham. Faber. 1972 (New edition)

Victorian Pottery
Hugh G. Wakefield. Herbert Jenkins. 1962

English Blue and White Porcelain of the Eighteenth Century
Bernard Watney. Faber. 1973 (New edition)

Continental ceramics

Italian Porcelain
Francesco Stazzi. George Weidenfeld and Nicolson. 1967

Italian Maiolica
Bernard Rackham. Faber. 1964

French Porcelain of the Eighteenth Century
W. B. Honey. Faber. 1972

French Faience
Arthur Lane. Faber. 1970 (New edition)

Greek Pottery
Arthur Lane. Faber. 1971 (New edition)

Animals in Pottery and Porcelain
John P. Cushion. Studio Vista. 1974

Oriental ceramics

Chinese Porcelain
Anthony du Boulay. Octopus Books Limited. 1973

Early Chinese Pottery and Porcelain
Basil Gray. Faber. 1953

Later Chinese Porcelain
Soame Jenyns. Faber. 1972

Korean Pottery
W. B. Honey. Faber. 1952

Japanese Porcelain
Soame Jenyns. Faber. 1965

Japanese Pottery
Soame Jenyns. Faber. 1971

Allied subjects

The Artist's Handbook of Materials and Techniques
Ralph Mayer. Fourth Edition. Viking Press. 1970; Faber. 1982
  Mr. Mayer's book is a mine of information on all artist's materials, including a chapter on pigments.

The Book of a Hundred Hands
George Bridgman. Dover Publications. 1972
  Invaluable for the restorer wishing to draw and model hands accurately.

Modelling and Sculpture
Albert Toft. Seeley Service. 1950; Macmillan, New York. 1950
  A very useful book.

Miscellaneous

Handbook of Pottery and Porcelain Marks
J. P. Cushion and W. B. Honey. Faber. 1965 (New edition)

Pocket Book of British Ceramic Marks
J. P. Cushion. Faber. 1976 (New edition)

Pocket Book of German Ceramic Marks
J. P. Cushion. Faber. 1961

Pocket Book of French and Italian Ceramic Marks
J. P. Cushion. Faber. 1965

Forgeries, Fakes and Reproductions
George Savage. Barrie and Rockliffe. 1963 (U.S., Praeger, 1964)

Adhesives Guide
Joyce Hurd. British Scientific Instruments Research Association. 'Sira', South Hill, Chislehurst, Kent.

Synthetic Materials used in The Conservation of Cultural Property
Published by the International Centre for the Study and Restoration of Cultural Property, Rome-256, Via Cavour. 1963

Handbook of Organic and Industrial Solvents
Published by American Mutual Insurance Alliance, 20 North Wacker Drive, Chicago, Illinois 60606.

Design for Scientific Conservation of Antiquities
Robert M. Organ. Smithsonian Institution. 1968
Concerned with the design of, and equipment for, the museum laboratory, but contains much useful information for the restorer.

Science for Conservators
A specialist series for non-scientists. Available from The Conservation Section, Crafts Council, 12 Waterloo Place, London SW1Y 4AU.

Alphabetical list of materials, tools and equipment

Names of suppliers have been abbreviated: see list of suppliers for correct mode of address

	U.K. suppliers	U.S. suppliers
Ablebond 342-1 epoxy resin, parts A and B.	Cons. Materials	Cons. Materials
Acetone	Joel; Hopkins	City Chemical; hardware; Cons. Materials
Acrylic colours, W&N (U.K.), Hyplar (U.S.)	Winsor; artist's shops	Artist's shops
Acryloid B48N	*See* Bedacryl 122X	Cons. Materials
Agate burnisher	Winsor; artist's shops	N.Y. Central; Cons. Materials
Airbrush	DeVilbiss; Colour Sprays	Cons. Materials; Thayer & Chandler
Alcohol, denatured ethyl	*See* methylated spirits (industrial)	City Chemical; Hardware; Cons. Materials
Ammonia 880 (U.K.), 28% (U.S.)	Joel; Hopkins	City Chemical; Cons. Materials
Araldite, Two-Tube pack	Hardware stores	*See* Devcon '2-ton'
Araldite, AY 103 with Hardener HY 956	Ciba; Joel	*See* Ablebond 342-1

Arkansas stone, Fine	*See* Carborundum stone	Allcraft; Abbey; Uptown; Cons. Materials
Aron Alpha	*See* Loctite IS 496	Cons. Materials
Attapulgus Clay	*See* Sepiolite	Cons. Materials
Automotive lacquer thinner, high aromatic	*See* Chintex Thinner	Automotive supplies
Barytes powder	Joel	Cons. Materials; City Chemical
Bedacryl 122X	Joel	*See* Acryloid B48N
Bottles, plastic	Boots	A.I.N.
Bronze powders	Robertson	N.Y. Central; Pearl; Cons. Materials
Brushes, artist's quality sable	Winsor; artist's shops	N.Y. Central; Flax; Cons. Materials; Brown; artist's stores
Brush, wire	Walsh	Uptown; jeweller's suppliers
Butcher's Wax	*See* Slipwax release agent	Supermarkets
Callipers	Walsh	N.Y. Central, Sculpture Hse, Sculpture Services
Carbide instruments, burs	Ash	Cons. Materials

	U.K. suppliers	U.S. suppliers
Carborundum stick (U.K.), slip (U.S.) triangular-shaped	Walsh; Tiranti	Uptown; Abbey
Carborundum stone, fine	Walsh; Tiranti	*See* Arkansas stone
Cellosolve (acetate) solvent	Hopkins; Joel	City Chemical; Cons. Materials
Celluloid	Craft and hobby shops	Craft and hobby shops
Chinaglaze Clear Gloss	Joel	Cons. Materials
China marking pencils	*See* Volatile crayons	N.Y. Central
Chintex clear glaze, brush cleaner	Joel	Cons. Materials
Chintex thinner	Joel	*See* Automotive thinner
Compressor	DeVilbiss; Colour Sprays	N.Y. Central; Flax; Allcraft
Creams, barrier and cleansing (for the skin)	Boots; Tiranti	Pharmacy
Cyanoacrylate; Loctite IS496 (U.K.), Aron Alpha (U.S.)	Joel	Cons. Materials
De-ionizer (and replacement cartridges)	Joel	*See* Demineralizer
Demineralizer, Illco-Way (Universal Model)	*See* De-Ionizer	Fisher

Dental impression compound		
Paribar (U.K.), Mercaptan-MIM (U.S.)	Ash (MIM available Joel)	Cons. Materials
Dental tools, hand	Ash	Rower; Arista
De-Solv 292 (U.K.) Epoxy Dissolver (U.S.)	Joel	Cons. Materials
Devcon '2-ton' Epoxy	*See* Araldite Two-Tube pack	
Diamond-tipped and carbide instruments	Ash	Cons. Materials
Distilled water	Boots	City Chemical or supermarkets
Dividers	Walsh	Uptown; N.Y. Central; Flax
Drill, flexible-shaft	Buck; Ash; Joel	Cons. Materials
End cutters	*See* Top cutters	Abbey; Uptown; Cons. Materials
Ferroclene 389	Joel	*See* Naval Jelly
File, large medium cut	Walsh	Abbey; Uptown; Allcraft
Flat long-nosed pliers	Walsh	Abbey; Uptown; Cons. Materials
Flexigrit A-400	Joel	Cons. Materials
Folding pocket magnifier, X10	Walsh	Abbey, Uptown; Cons. Materials

	U.K. suppliers	**U.S. suppliers**
Gauge, Stubs pattern (for measuring diameters of wire)	Walsh; Buck	Abbey; Uptown
Glass, off-cuts	Suppliers of plate glass	Suppliers of plate glass
Gloves, disposable	Boots; Joel	Cons. Materials
Gold	*See* Tablet gold and transfer gold leaf	
Goggles, Duralair (U.K.), Eastern Safety (U.S.)	Tiranti; Joel	Cons. Materials
Gravers	Walsh	Allcraft
Hacksaw blades	Buck	Abbey; Uptown
Hydrogen peroxide 100 vol. (U.K.), 30–35% (U.S.)	Joel; Hopkins	City Chemical; Cons. Materials
Kaolin powder	Joel; Boots	City Chemical; Cons. Materials
Lamp, flexible arm	Walsh	Artist's stores; jeweller's suppliers; Manhattan
Maimeri Colours	—	Cons. Materials
Magnesium Trisilicate	*See* Sepiolite	Cons. Materials
Magnifying glass, X10	Walsh	N.Y. Central; Cons. Materials

Marble flour (U.K.), powder (U.S.)	Joel; Ciba
Matting agent, Gasil (23C U.K.), Cabosil (U.S.)	Joel
Methylated spirits, industrial (with licence)	*See* Alcohol
Methylene chloride	City Chemical
Methyl ethyl Keytone	City Chemical
Mixing saucers	Artist's stores
Modelling tools, boxwood	Tiranti
Modelling tools, wire	Tiranti
Moulds, rubber latex	*See* Qualitex or Revultex
Moulds, silicone rubber	*See* Rhodorsil RTV 11504A *or* Silastomer 9161
Naval Jelly (rust remover)	*See* Ferroclene 389
Needle files	Walsh
Nitromors	Joel; hardware

Cons. Materials	
Cons. Materials	
See Alcohol	
City Chemical	
City Chemical	
Artist's stores	
Sculpture House; Sculpture Services; Cons. Materials	
Sculpture House; Sculpture Services; Cons. Materials	
See Pliatex	
See Silastic 3110	
Hardware	
Abbey; Uptown; Cons. Materials	
See Methylene chloride (also ask Cons. Materials for Nitromors)	

	U.K. suppliers	U.S. suppliers
Non-ionic detergent, Synperonic NDB (U.K.), Triton X100 (U.S.)	Joel	City Chemical; Cons. Materials
Oil colours, artist's quality	Winsor; artist's shops	Artist's shops; Cons. Materials
Palette knives	Artist's shops	Artist's shops; Cons. Materials
Phenthin 83	Joel	Cons. Materials
Pin vice	Walsh	Abbey; Allcraft
Plaster of Paris, dental quality	Boots; Tiranti	See Snow White No. 1
Plasticine (U.K.), Plastelina, Roma Italian, No. 2 White (U.S.)	Tiranti; Joel; artist's shops	Sculpture House; Cons. Materials
Pliatex	See Qualitex or Revultex	Sculpture House
Polish, Simoniz	Garages	Garages; hardware
Polyester Resin, Sintolit transparent	Joel	Cons. Materials
Polyfilla	Joel; hardware	Cons. Materials
Polyfilla, Fine Surface	Joel; hardware	Cons. Materials
Polyvinyl acetate emulsion (P.V.A.) Vinamul 6815 (U.K.), C M Bond M-3 (U.S.)	Joel	Cons. Materials
Polyvinyl Alcohol Resin	Joel	Cons. Materials

Powder pigments	Robertson; Winsor; artist's shops	Cons. Materials
Qualitex P.V.	Joel	See Pliatex
Renaissance Wax	Tiranti; Joel	Cons. Materials
Respirator, Duralair (U.K.), Eastern Safety (U.S.)	Tiranti; Joel	Cons. Materials
Revultex	Bellman Ivey	See Pliatex
Rhodorsil RTV 1 1504A	Joel	See Silastic 3110
Riffler files	Walsh	Allcraft
Round-nosed pliers	Walsh	Cons. Materials
Ruler, steel	Buck; Walsh	N.Y. Central
Scales, gramme	Walsh	Cons. Materials
Scalpel blades and holders 3 and 4	Joel; Bell	Cons. Materials
Sepiolite (U.K.), Magnesium Trisilicate (or Attapulgus Clay) (U.S.)	Joel	City Chemical; Cons. Materials
Sheet brass, fine gauge	Smith	Cons. Materials
Silastomer 9161 with Catalyst N 9162	Tiranti; Hopkins	See Silastic 3110
Slipwax release agent	Joel	See Butcher's Wax

	U.K. suppliers	**U.S. suppliers**
Solvol Autosol	Tiranti; hardware	Cons. Materials
Spatula, metal	Tiranti	Sculpture House; Cons. Materials
Stoddard solvent	*See* White spirit	Cons. Materials
Tablet gold	Robertson	N.Y. Central; Cons. Materials
Talc	Joel	City Chemical
Tiles	Hardware	Giurdanella
Titanium dioxide powder	Joel; Winsor	City Chemical; Cons. Materials
Top cutters	Walsh	*See* End Cutters
Tracing paper	Artist's shops	Artist's shops
Transfer gold leaf	Robertson	N.Y. Central; Cons. Materials
Turpentine, artist's quality	Artist's shops	Artist's shops
Tweezers, finely pointed	Walsh	Brookstone; Uptown; Abbey
Tweezers, heavy duty	Walsh	Uptown; Abbey
Vice, small metal	Buck; Walsh	Abbey; Uptown
Volatile crayons	Wengers	*See* China marking pencils

White spirit | *See* Stoddard solvent
Wire, electrical (U.K.), tie wire (U.S.) | Elm; hardware
Wire, half hard brass | Cons. Materials
Wire, soft stainless steel | Cons. Materials
Xylene | City Chemical; Cons. Materials

Joel
Electrical suppliers
Smith; Ormiston
Renown
Joel; Hopkins

Alphabetical lists of suppliers

U.K. suppliers

Claudius Ash Sons & Co. Ltd., 26 Broadwick St., London W1A 2AD

John Bell and Croyden, 50 Wigmore St., London W1H 0AU

Bellman Ivey Carter & Co., 358A, Grand Drive, Wimbledon, London SW20 9NQ

Boots Company Ltd., 1 Thane Road West, Nottingham NG2 3AA

Buck and Ryan Ltd., 101 Tottenham Court Road, London W1P 0DY

Ciba-Geigy Ltd., Duxford, Cambridge CB2 4QA

Colour Sprays Ltd., 62 Southwark Bridge Road, London SE1 0AS

The DeVilbiss Company Ltd., 47 Holborn Viaduct, London EC1A 2PB

Hopkins and Williams, Freshwater Road, Chadwell Heath, Romford, Essex RM1 1HB

Frank W. Joel, Museum Laboratory & Archeological Supplies, Unit 5, Old Meadow Road, Hardwick Industrial Estate, King's Lynn, Norfolk PE30 4HH

P. Ormiston and Sons Ltd., Broughton Road, London W13 8QW

Renown Special Steels Ltd., Eley Estate, Nobel Road, Edmonton; 273 Green Lane, Palmer's Green, London N18 3BH

C. Robertson & Co. Ltd., Parkway, London NW1 7PP

J. Smith and Sons (Clerkenwell) Ltd., 42–54 St. John's Square, Clerkenwell, London EC1P 1ER

Alec Tiranti Ltd., 70 High Street, Theale, Reading, Berks RG7 5AR; 21 Goodge Place, London W1P 2AJ (catalogue)

Union Carbide UK Ltd., Chemical Division, P.O. Box 2LR, 8 Grafton Street, London W1A 2LR

H. S. Walsh, 12–16 Clerkenwell Road, London EC1M 5PL (catalogue)

Wengers Ltd., Etruria Works, Garner St., Stoke-on-Trent, Staffordshire ST4 7BQ (catalogue)

Winsor and Newton, 51 Rathbone Place, London W1P 1AB

U.S. suppliers

Abbey Materials Corp., 116 W. 29th St., New York, N.Y. 10001 (catalogue)

A.I.N. Plastics, 300 Park Ave. South, New York. N.Y. 10010

Allcraft Tool & Supply Co., 22 W. 48th St., New York. N.Y. 10036

Arista Surgical Supply Co. Inc., 67 Lexington Ave., New York, N.Y. 10010

Brookstone Company, 'Hard to Find Tools', 121 Vose Farm Road, Peterborough. N.H. 03458 (mail order catalogue)

Arthur Brown, 2 W. 46th St., New York. N.Y. 10036 (catalogue)

City Chemical, 132 W. 22nd St., New York, N.Y. 10011

Conservation Materials Ltd. Box 2884, Sparks, NV 89431. (excellent catalogue, distributor of Ablebond 342-1 *worldwide*)

Fisher Scientific*, 52 Fadem Road, Springfield, N.J. 07081 (this branch serves New Jersey and New York)

Sam Flax, 25 E. 28th St., New York, N.Y. 10016

---

*Fisher Scientific (who also sell chemicals) have branches in the following cities: Atlanta, Ga.; Boston, Mass.; Chicago, Ill.; Cincinnati, O.; Cleveland, O.; Houston, Texas; Philadelphia, Pa.; Pittsburgh, Pa.; St. Louis, Mo.; Washington, D.C.

The Foredom Electric Company, Bethel, Conn. 06801 (catalogues, addresses of retailers)

Giurdanella Bros., 4 Bond St., New York, N.Y. 10002

Manhattan Sales Co., 17 E. 16th St., New York, N.Y. 10003

Michael's of San Francisco, 314 Sutter Street, San Francisco, Cal. 94105

New York Central Supply Co., 62 Third Ave., New York, N.Y. 10003 (catalogue)

Pearl Paint Co., 308 Canal St., New York, N.Y. 10013

Rower Dental Supply, 331–337 W. 44th St., New York, N.Y. 10036

Scientific Glass Apparatus Co. Inc.*, 735 Broad St., Bloomfield, N.J. 07003 (for New York and New Jersey)

Sculpture House, 38 E. 30th St., New York, N.Y. 10016 (mail order catalogue)

Sculpture Services, Inc., 9 E. 19th St., New York, N.Y. 10003 (catalogue)

Thyer and Chandler Inc., 442 North Wells St., Chicago, Ill. 60610

Uptown Material House, 50 W. 47th St., New York, N.Y. 10017 (catalogue)

Note: The two main distributors, Frank W. Joel in the U.K. and Conservation Materials Ltd. in the U.S. keep up to date with new materials and will try to stock things requested by their customers. They will answer questions and give as much information as possible. By purchasing most tools and materials from one distributor, the restorer can save time and money. Also, many manufacturers no longer supply small quantities.

Jeweller's supplies
Frei-Borel, 760 Market St., San Francisco, Cal. 94102

---

*Scientific Glass Apparatus Co. Inc. (who also sell chemicals) have branches in the following cities: Boston, Mass.; Chicago, Ill.; Danbury, Conn.; Los Angeles, Cal.; Philadelphia, Pa.; Washington, D.C.

Index

Ablebond 342-1 epoxy resin, 29, 54–5, 59–60, 62, 68–70, 75–7, 100–2, 108, 114, 118, 130
acetone, 31, 39, 41–3, 53, 56, 109, 116, 121–2, 125, 129
Acryloid B48N *see* Bedacryl 122X
adhesives, 29–30, 45–58, 132; removal of, 39–41
ammonia, 31, 39–43, 107, 122
Araldite AY 103 (and Hardener HY 956), 29, 54–5, 59–60, 62, 68–70, 75–7, 100–2, 108, 114, 118, 130
Araldite (Two-Tube), 29, 30, 45–54, 59, 62, 69, 75–6
Aron Alpha *see* Cyanoacrylate resin
Attapulgus Clay *see* Sepiolite

baking, 72, 81–2, 85–6, 95–6, 113, 132
barytes powder, 30, 59, 77
Bedacryl 122X, 33, 80–2, 86, 95, 97–8, 109, 114, 118, 123, 128
bonding, 45–58, 132
breaks, multiple, 50–4
bronze powders, 34, 96
burnishing, 95–6, 114, 132
Butcher's Wax, *see* Slipwax

Cabosil *see* Gasil 23 C
Cellosolve (acetate) solvent, 33, 80, 86, 118, 123, 128

cellulose adhesives, removal of, 41
Chinaglaze, 33, 80–2, 93, 95, 102, 109, 114; solvent, 33, 80, 102–3, 109, 134
china mending, examples of: Chelsea plate, 106–10; Creamware centre piece, 116–20; Derby vase, 111–15; porcelain pastille burner, 99–105; T'ang pottery, 125–9; tin-glazed earthenware cup, 121–4
Chintex, 33, 80–2, 85, 93, 95–6
chips, filling in, 61–2
clamps, removal of, 42–3
clay, firing of, 17
cleaning and preparation, 39–44
clothing, protective, 36
colour, sense of, 16
colour-matching, 63–4, 79–92, 102–5, 109–10, 118–20, 123–4, 128, 130–2
colours: acrylic, artist's oil, dry powder, 33–4, 45–6, 63–4, 75, 80, 83–5, 88, 90, 92, 95, 103–5, 109–10, 115, 118–19, 122–4, 127, 130–1
conservation, defined, 15, 132
crackle, 90–1, 132
cracks, filling in, 60
crazing, 90–1, 133
Cyanoacrylate resin 29–30, 55–6

decoration, 89–92, 102–5, 109–10, 133

detergent, safe, 43
Devcon '2-ton' see Araldite
   (Two-Tube)
dexterity, manual, necessity for,
   15
dowelling, 53, 73–6, 114, 128,
   133
drilling, 66, 73–8, 100, 133

Epotek 301 (and Hardener), see
   Araldite AY 103
epoxy resin adhesives, removal
   of, 39–40
equipment, list of, 140–7
ethyl alcohol, see methylated
   spirits
eyes, protection of, 36

Ferroclene, 32, 43
fillers, 30–1
filling in, 59–78, 133
furniture, 18–19

Gasil matting agent, 33–5, 118,
   130–1
gilding, 34, 93–6, 133
glaze mediums, 80–92
glazes, including solvents,
   paints and pigments, 33–4
glazing, 80–97, 102–5, 109–10,
   114–15, 119, 123–4, 127–8,
   130–1, 133
glues, removal of, 40
goggles, 26, 36
gold leaf, 34, 93–5, 115
gold, tablet, see tablet gold

handling, importance of proper,
   16
hydrogen peroxide, 31, 41–3,
   107, 116, 122

join, sprung or warped, 49–50,
   134

kaolin powder, 30, 59, 77, 100,
   108, 114, 118, 123, 126
keying, 46–8, 55–6, 72, 111–14,
   126, 133

labels, importance of, 28–9;
   removal of, 43–4
lacquer thinner, automotive, 33
lustre ware, 96

magnesium trisilicate, see
   Sepiolite
Maimeri colours, 34
marble flour, 30, 59–63, 100,
   108, 114
materials, cleaning and
   preparation, 31–2; lists of,
   28–35, 140–7; modelling and
   moulding, 32–3; necessity for
   good quality, 15
Mercaptan, see Paribar
methylated spirits, 29, 31,
   45–6, 49, 53–4, 60, 62, 101,
   108
methylene chloride, see
   Nitromors
modelling, 68–9, 76–8, 111–14,
   133
moulds, making, 61–2, 64–73;
   rubber latex, 32–3, 66–70,
   100, 107–9, 117–18, 135;
   silicone rubber, 33, 70–3,
   111–14

Naval Jelly, see Ferroclene
Nitromors, 32, 39–41, 100, 116,
   125–6

painting, airbrush, 16, 79,
   86–9, 92, 114–15, 128, 130–1,
   134; hand, 16, 79–81, 82–6,
   89–92, 102–5, 109–10,
   118–20, 123–4, 128, 130–1,
   134

paints and varnishes, removal
of, 41
Paribar, 33, 64–6
patience, necessity for, 15
Phenthin 83 solvent *see*
Chinaglaze
pinning, 76–8, 100, 134
plaster of Paris, 30, 62, 67, 117,
123, 126–7, 135
Plasticine, 32, 49–53, 61–5,
68–73, 102, 108, 111–13, 126,
135
Pliatex, *see* Qualitex *or*
Revultex
polishing, 97–8, 134
Polyfilla, 30, 62–4, 126–7
polyvinyl acetate emulsion
(P.V.A.), 29, 56–7, 122–3,
126
protection of clothing, eyes,
skin, 36

Qualitex PV rubber latex, 66–8

reinforcing, 73–6, 134
repair project, choice of first,
37–8
respirator, 26, 36
restoration, defined, 15, 134
Revultex rubber latex, 66–8
Rhodorsil Silicone Rubber, 33,
66, 70–1
rivets, removal of, 42–3
Roma Plastelina, *see* Plasticine
rubber cement, removal of,
40–1

sand box, 48–53, 55, 57, 75–6,
126, 134
sanding, 60, 62–6, 78, 82–3, 90,
98, 102, 109–10, 114, 118,
123–4, 127–8, 130–1, 134
Scotch tape, 45, 49–57, 62, 67,

100, 108, 114, 118, 126
sensibility, necessity for, 15
Sepiolite, 32, 35
shellac, removal of, 40
Silastic 3110 *see* Rhodosil
Silastomer silicone rubber, 33,
66, 70–1
Simoniz, 35, 97, 120
skin, protection of, 36
Slipwax release agent, 35, 67,
72, 113–14, 117
Solvol Autosol, 35, 66, 78, 97,
109
Stoddard Solvent *see* white spirit
stains, removal of, 41–3
strapping, 49, 100, 114, 135
surface finishing, 35, 97–8
Synperonic NDB, 32, 43, 106

tablet gold, 34, 95–6
talc, 35, 61, 63, 67–9, 72, 100,
113, 118
titanium dioxide powder, 30,
45–6, 54–5, 59–60, 75, 77, 82,
100, 108, 114, 118
tools, lists of, 20–7, 140–7
Triton X100, *see* Synperonic
NDB

ventilation, 18
Vinamul 6815, *see* polyvinyl
acetate (P.V.A.)

water, distilled, 31, 39–43,
56–7, 61–3, 106–7, 116, 122,
125–6
wax, modelling, 32, 67–9, 111
waxes, 35
white spirit, 32
work room, 18–19

Xylene, 33, 80, 86, 118, 123,
128